MONSTER MISSION

EVA IBBOTSON

MACMILLAN CHILDREN'S BOOKS

First published 1999 by Macmillan Children's Books

This edition published 2014 by Macmillan Children's Books
an imprint of Pan Macmillan
a division of Macmillan Publishers Limited
20 New Wharf Road, London N1 9RR
Associated companies throughout the world
www.panmacmillan.com

ISBN 978-1-4472-6569-6

1 3 5 7 9 8 6 4 2

A CIP catalogue record for this book is available from
the British Library.

Typeset by SX Composing DTP, Rayleigh, Essex
Printed and bound by CPI Group (UK) Ltd, Croydon CR0 4YY

To my husband, who really cared about
unusual creatures

Chapter One

Kidnapping children is not a good idea. All the same, sometimes it has to be done.

Aunt Etta and Aunt Coral and Aunt Myrtle were not natural kidnappers. For one thing, they were getting old and kidnapping is hard work; for another, though they looked a little odd, they were very caring people. They cared for their ancient father and for their shrivelled cousin Sybil who lived in a cave and tried to foretell the future – and most particularly they cared for the animals on the island on which they lived, many of which were quite unusual.

Some of the creatures that made their way to the Island had come far across the ocean to be looked after, and lately the aunts had felt that they could not go on much longer without help. And 'help' didn't mean grown-ups who were set in their ways. Help meant children who were young and strong and willing to learn.

So on a cool blustery day in April the three aunts gathered round the kitchen table and decided to go ahead. Some children had to be found and they had to be brought to the island, and kidnapping seemed the only sensible way to do it.

'That way we can choose the ones that are suitable,' said Aunt Etta. She was the eldest; a tall, bony woman who did fifty press-ups before breakfast and had a small but not at all unpleasant moustache on her upper lip.

The others looked out of the window at the soft green turf, the sparkling sea, and sighed, thinking of what had to be done. The sleeping powders, the drugged hamburgers, the bags and sacks and cello cases they would need to carry the children away in . . .

'Will they scream and wriggle, do you suppose?' asked Aunt Myrtle, who was the youngest. She suffered from headaches and hated noise.

'No, of course not. They'll be unconscious,' said Aunt Etta. 'Flat out. I don't like it any more than you do,' she went on, 'but you saw the programme on TV last week.'

The others nodded. When they first came to the Island they hadn't had any electricity, but after his hundredth birthday their father's toes had started to turn blue because not enough blood got to his feet and they had ordered a generator so that he could have an electric blanket. After that they thought they might as well have an electric kettle, and then a TV.

But the TV had been a mistake because of the nature programmes. Nature programmes always end badly. First you see the hairy-nosed wombats frisking about with their babies and then five minutes before the end you hear that there are only twelve breeding pairs left in the whole of Australia. Or there are pictures of the harlequin frogs of Costa Rica croaking away on their lily leaves and the next minute you are told that they're doomed because their swamps are being drained. Worst of all are the

2

rainforests. The aunts could never see a programme about the rainforests without crying, and last week there had been a particularly bad one with wicked people burning and slashing the trees, and pictures of the monkeys and the jaguars rushing away in terror.

'What if *we* became extinct?' Aunt Coral had wondered, blowing her nose. 'Not just the wombats and the harlequin frogs and the jaguars, but *us*.'

The others had seen the point at once. If a whole rainforest can become extinct why not three elderly ladies? And if they became extinct what would happen to their work and who would care for the creatures that came to the Island in search of comfort and of care?

There was another thing which bothered the aunts. Lately the animals that came to the Island simply wouldn't go away again. Long after they were healed they stayed on – it was almost as if they knew something – and that made more and more work for the aunts. There was no doubt about it, help had to be brought in, and quickly.

So now they were deciding what to do.

'How do we find the *right* children?' asked Myrtle as she looked longingly out at the point where the seals were resting. One of the seals, Herbert, was her special friend and she would very much rather have been out there playing her cello to him and singing her songs.

'We shall become *Aunts*,' said Etta firmly, settling her spectacles on her long nose.

The others looked at her in amazement. 'But we *are* aunts,' they said. 'How can we *become* them?'

This was true. There had been five sisters who had come to the Island with their father many years ago. They had found a ruined house and deserted beaches with only the footprints of sandpipers and dunlins on the sand, and barnacle geese resting on the way from Greenland, and the seals, quite unafraid, coming out of the water to have their pups.

They had started to repair the house, and planted a garden, and then one day they had found an oiled seabird washed up on a rock . . . Only it turned out not to be an oiled seabird. It was oiled all right, but it was something quite different – and after that they realized that they had been called to the Island by a Higher Power and that they had found their life's work.

But one of the sisters, Betty, had not cared for the Island. She hated the wind and the rain and the fish scales in her tea and the eider ducklings nesting in her bedroom slippers and she had gone away and got married to a tax inspector in Newcastle upon Tyne and now she lived in a house with three kinds of toilet freshener in the loo, and sprays to make her armpits smell nice, and not a fish scale in sight.

But the point was that she had two children. They were horrible, but they were children. She called the boy Boo-Boo and the girl Little One (though they had proper names of course). But horrible though they were, they were children and because of this her sisters had become aunts since all you have to do to become an aunt is have nephews and nieces.

Which is why now the sisters looked so surprised and said: 'But we *are* aunts.'

'Not that kind,' said Etta impatiently. 'I mean the

4

kind that live in an office or an agency and call themselves things like *Useful Aunts* or *Universal Aunts* or *Aunts Inc.* – the kind that parents pay to take their children to school and to the dentist, or to sit with them when they are ill.'

'Why don't the parents do it themselves?' asked Myrtle.

'Because they're too busy. People used to have real aunts and grandmothers and cousins to do it all, but now families are too small and real aunts go to dances and have boyfriends,' said Etta, snorting.

Coral nodded her head. She was the arty one, a large plump person who fed the chickens in a feather boa and interesting jewellery, and at night by the light of the moon she danced the tango.

'It's a good idea,' she said. 'You would be able to pick and choose the children – you don't want to end up with a Boo-Boo or a Little One.'

'Yes, but if the parents are truly fond of the children we shouldn't do it,' said Myrtle, pushing back her long grey hair.

'Well of course not,' said Etta. 'We don't want a hue and cry.'

'But if the children are nice the parents *would* be fond of them,' said Myrtle. 'And if they aren't we don't want them either.'

Etta sniffed. 'You'd be surprised. There are children all over the place whose parents don't know how lucky they are.'

They went on talking for a long time but no one could think of anything better than Etta's plan – not if the position of the Island was to be kept secret, and there was nothing more important than that.

5

There was one more aunt who would have been useful – not the one with the three kinds of toilet freshener, who was no use for anything – but Aunt Dorothy, who was next in age to Etta and would have been just the sort of person to have on a kidnapping expedition. But Dorothy was in prison in Hong Kong. She had gone out there to stop a restaurant owner from serving pangolin steaks – pangolins are beautiful creatures and are getting rare and should never be eaten – and Dorothy had got annoyed and hit the restaurant owner on the head with his own wok, and they had put her in prison. She was due out in a month but in the meantime only the three of them could go on the mission and they weren't at all sure about Myrtle because she was not very good out in the world and when she was away she always pined for Herbert.

'Are you sure you wouldn't rather stay behind, Myrtle?' said Coral now. But Myrtle had decided to be brave and said she thought that she should come along and do her bit.

'Only we won't say anything to Daddy,' said Etta. 'After all, kidnapping is a crime and he might worry.'

Captain Harper lived upstairs in a big bed with a telescope, looking out to sea. They had mostly given up telling him things. For one thing, he was stone deaf so that explaining anything took a very long time, and for another, as soon as he saw anybody he started telling them stories about what life had been like when he was a boy. They were good stories but every single aunt had heard them about three hundred times so they didn't hang around if they could help it.

6

But they did go and tell the Sybil. She was the old cousin who had come to the Island soon after them. Sybil was bookish and one day she had read a book about Greek mythology and about a person called *the* Sybil (not just Sybil) who was a prophetess and could foretell the future. So she had started prophesying about the weather, mumbling on about depressions over Iceland and the wind-chill factor and really she didn't get it wrong much more often than the weathermen on the telly. Then she had gone on to other things, and had gone to live in a cave with bats because that was where prophetesses were supposed to live, and had stopped washing because she said washing would weaken her powers, so that she was another person one did not visit for too long.

When the aunts told her that they were going to the mainland to kidnap some children the Sybil got quite excited. Her face turned blue and her hair began to stand on end and for a moment they hoped that she was going to tell them something important about the journey.

But it turned out that what she was foreseeing was squally showers, and what she said was 'take seasick pills', which they had decided to do anyway for the boat.

They still had to make sure that their cook, who was called Art, knew exactly what to do while they were away on their mission. Art was an escaped convict who had been washed up in a rowing boat on their shore. He had killed a man when he was young, and now he wouldn't kill anything with arms or legs or eyes – not even a shrimp – but he made excellent porridge. Then they gathered together all the things they would need: chloroform and sleeping powders and anaesthetizing darts which they used for stunning animals that were injured so that they could set their limbs. All of them had things to carry the children away in: Aunt Etta had a canvas holdall and Aunt Coral had a tin trunk with holes bored into it and Aunt Myrtle had her cello case. As they waited for the wind to change so that they could sail the *Peggoty* to the next island and catch the steamer, they were terribly excited.

It was a long and difficult journey – many years ago the army had tried to use the Island for experiments in radio signals and so as to keep its position secret they had changed the maps and forbidden boats to come near it. In the end they hadn't used it after all but it was still a forgotten place and the aunts meant to see that it stayed that way.

'Of course it won't be a real kidnap because we shan't ask the parents for a ransom,' said Etta.

'It'll be more of a child snatch,' Coral agreed.

But whether it was a kidnap or a child snatch, it was still dangerous and wicked, and as they waved goodbye to the Island their hearts were beating very fast.

Chapter Two

By the time she was ten years old Minette had made the journey between London and Edinburgh forty-seven times. Forty-seven station buffet sandwiches; forty-seven visits to the loo on the train and forty-seven stomach-aches because changing families always churned up her insides.

Minette's father lived in Edinburgh in a tall grey house and was a Professor of Grammar. Minette's mother lived in a flat in London and was an actress – at least she would have been if anyone had given her any work. They had been separated since Minette was three years old and they hated each other with a bitter and deadly hatred.

'Tell that louse of a father of yours that he's late with his money again,' was the sort of message that Minette's mother usually sent as she took her daughter to King's Cross to put her on the train to Edinburgh. Or:

'No doubt your mother is still running a doss-house for drunken actors,' her father would say as he fetched her from the train.

Minette never gave her parents these messages. She made up polite friendly messages for them to send each other but neither her mother nor her father believed her when she delivered them. And on the journey, which took five hours when she first began

9

to travel, Minette would look out of the window searching for houses where she and her mother and her father would live together one day like an ordinary family with a cat and a canary and a dog. For it went on hurting her, hurting and hurting – not that her parents were separated; lots of children she knew had separated parents – but that they hated each other so much.

On these journeys Minette was usually put in the charge of an aunt. The aunt came from an office called *Useful Aunts* and what she was like was important because if she talked all the time or wanted to play silly games, Minette couldn't give her mind to finding houses for her parents to live in, or imagining beautiful scenes where she was run over and taken to hospital and her mother and father rushed to her bedside and looked at each other over their daughter's bleeding body and found that they loved each other after all.

Then as she got up to go on her forty-eighth journey, Minette suddenly realized that it didn't matter *what* kind of aunt they sent to take her because she had given up hope. Her parents would always hate each other and she would spend the rest of her life travelling from London to Edinburgh and back again, never quite knowing which was her home or where she properly belonged.

And as though someone Up There had heard her, they sent her that day a quite extraordinary aunt.

She was so unlike the other aunts she had travelled with that both Minette and her mother stopped dead as they came up to where she waited, by the bookstall on Platform One of King's Cross Station.

'Are you . . . ?' began Mrs Danby.

The woman nodded. She was very tall with a small moustache and carried a large holdall which smelled slightly of fish.

'I am your aunt,' she said in a deep voice and pointed to her lapel on which there was a label saying *Unusual Aunts* and above that the words 'My name is Etta'.

If Minette's mother hadn't been in a hurry to go to the cinema with her latest boyfriend she might have asked more questions. After all an *Unusual Aunt* is not quite the same as a *Useful* one, but as it was she handed over the money for the tickets and Minette's lunch, took the cigarette out of her mouth long enough to kiss her daughter, and went away.

And presently Minette and the aunt sat opposite each other in one of those old-fashioned compartments which have no corridor and watched the train make its way through the London suburbs.

Aunt Etta and her sisters had had a hard week in London. They found a boarding house full of people like themselves – aunt-like persons who had come to town to show their pug dogs at dog shows or go to meetings about setting up retirement homes for ancient donkeys. But they hated the noise and the traffic and the dirty air, and they did not find it easy to get taken on by an agency.

Even when Etta got her label and was sent out on jobs, the children she was given were unspeakable. She took a little boy on a trip down the river who spent the whole time stuffing himself with ice cream and popcorn and crisps and dropping the wrappers in the water. She was sent to take a small girl to have

11

her teeth cleaned and saw her bite the dentist's hand, and she sat with a whining brat called Tarquin Sterndale-Fish who had the measles.

So by the time she met Minette on King's Cross Station, Etta had begun to think that this kidnapping idea was pretty stupid. The world seemed to be full of Boo-Boos and Little Ones and it was better to become extinct, like the rainforests, than to bring such children to the Island.

Her first sight of Minette did not make her feel hopeful. The child had a crumpled, pinched sort of look; she was small for her age and very thin and looked as though she had been born tired. A wet and feeble child would be quite useless for the work that had to be done. She was also very stupidly dressed with a load of fluffy pom-poms in her long brown hair and a T-shirt which said *Pinch me and I'll squeal* – and a pink plastic handbag shaped like a heart dangled from her shoulder.

And if Aunt Etta did not like the look of Minette, Minette was not in the least keen on Aunt Etta.

For a while the two of them sat in silence. From time to time a drop of water fell from the canvas holdall that the aunt had put on the luggage rack on to her topknot of grey hair, but she did not seem to notice it.

'Is something leaking?' asked Minette.

The aunt looked up and shook her head. 'The canvas never seems to dry out properly. I use it to move seals about. Only pups of course; a full-grown seal would never fit inside.'

Minette began to be interested; her face lost its pinched and troubled look. 'Are you a vet, then?'

'Not exactly. But that does sort of come into it.'

There was another silence. Minette did not like to pry so she looked out of the window again. They were coming to the first of the dream houses which Minette had chosen to live in with her parents. It was an old station-master's house with hanging baskets of flowers and a little gable. And as though she read her thoughts, the aunt said: 'What a pleasant place to live in. There might be ghost trains going through at night with interesting spectres. That could liven things up.'

Minette stared at her. 'Do you believe in—'

'Of course,' said the aunt briskly. 'Certainly. I believe in almost everything, don't you?'

'My father says we mustn't believe anything we can't see or prove,' she said.

'Really?'

When they had been travelling for an hour, Minette opened her suitcase and became very busy. She had been wearing pink and orange socks with a border of Mickey Mice. Now she took them off and put on plain white ones. Then she removed the T-shirt which said *Pinch me and I'll squeal* and put on a navy-blue one with long sleeves and no writing at all. And lastly she put the dangling handbag back in the suitcase and took out a practical leather purse.

The aunt said nothing, watching as Minette changed from a trendy little dresser to a sensible old-fashioned schoolgirl.

But Minette had not finished. She took out her brush and comb, propped a mirror on her knees, and began to plait her hair into two long, tight pigtails.

'I always change here,' she explained, 'because

13

there's nothing interesting to look at out of the window. My father doesn't like clothes with writing on. Or funny socks. He thinks they're vulgar. And he hates untidy hair.'

'And when you come back you change back again – put on the pom-poms and unplait your hair?'

'Yes. My mother likes it loose.'

'And you? Which do you like?'

Minette sighed. 'I'd like it cut short.'

'Well I have some scissors here. Why don't we cut it?' She opened a very large handbag and took out a pair of scissors.

'Oh no! I couldn't. Then *both* of them would be angry.'

Aunt Etta shrugged and dropped the scissors back into her bag. 'Actually long hair can be useful.'

'How can it?'

'Oh for polishing things . . . oyster shells and suchlike. And if you fell into the water it would be something to get hold of.'

They had come to the second of Minette's dream houses, a low white house on the bend of a river with a willow tree and a garden sloping down to the water. But this time Minette did not see her mother and father taking tea together on the lawn. She heard her father saying, 'That willow must come down, it cuts off all the light,' – and her mother saying, 'If you cut that tree down I'll have you put in a mental home.'

And suddenly, for no reason, she told this strange woman about her endless journeys from her mother's tiny flat with its smell of face powder and curry from the takeaway downstairs, and the tights

14

dripping in the bathroom, to her father's cold, tidy, solemn house with its ticking grandfather clock. And about the silly dreams she'd had of bringing them together and the hopelessness of it all.

'Do you think there might be a third place? Not my father's house or my mother's flat but somewhere else – by the sea perhaps? And that one day I might find it?'

She drew back, suddenly frightened, because the fierce aunt was looking at her far too intently.

But Aunt Etta was nodding. 'Of course,' she said. 'Of course there is a third place. There is one for everybody. But it's no good filling it up with people from your old life. If you want to find the third place you must find it alone.'

'But I'm a child. I can't go and live alone.'

'Perhaps not. Not exactly, but you might be able to make a new start just the same if you had the courage.'

'I don't have courage,' said Minette firmly. 'I'm a coward.' It was one of the few things on which her parents agreed. 'I'm frightened of the dark and of diving off the top board and of being bullied.'

The train stopped at York and the aunt bought sandwiches off a trolley. 'Now I suggest you go and wash your hands and freshen up,' she said, 'because it's time we had our lunch. Which of these sandwiches would you like – egg and cress or cheese and tomato?'

'Cheese and tomato, please.'

If Minette had known what was going to happen as soon as she had gone she would have been very scared indeed. For out of the pocket of her long

15

navy-blue knickers the aunt took a little box with a brownish powder which she sprinkled carefully into the centre of the cheese and tomato sandwich. Then she unzipped the holdall and sat back in her seat with a very contented smile.

'My first one,' she murmured to herself. 'My very first one. Oh really, this is most exciting!' And then: 'I wonder how Coral is getting on?'

It had been much harder to get Coral to look like an Agency Aunt. She was the plump one who had been to art school when she was young, and she liked to stand out from the crowd, but she had done her best to look sensible. She only wore two necklaces and one pair of dangly earrings and the hand-painted squiggles on her robe and matching turban were *peaceful* squiggles, so that when she rang the bell of the big house in Mayfair she felt that she looked as aunt-like as she ever would.

The idea of fetching Hubert-Henry Mountjoy from his grandparents' London house and taking him back to his boarding school in Berkshire made Aunt Coral feel extremely glum.

Her first batch of children had been as bad as Etta's: a poisonous, podgy child who had tried to kick her shins, and a little boy who jumped on a beetle in the park. She was sure that Hubert-Henry Mountjoy would not be her cup of tea – a cold-eyed, snotty little aristo too big for his boots – and she had decided that if she caught him jumping on beetles she would wallop him hard and give up being an aunt and go home.

As she was shown into the Mountjoys' hall by a

toffee-nosed maid, she felt worse than ever. The house was huge and dark and cold; there was a big brass gong in one corner; paintings of dead Mountjoys with handlebar moustaches hung on the walls. She waited for her first sight of Hubert-Henry in his school uniform with the deepest gloom.

The door of the drawing room opened. A small boy came out, pushed forward by a tall, white-haired man who looked exactly like the men in the portraits except that he wasn't dead – and her mouth dropped very slightly open.

Hubert-Henry was small and lightly built with jet-black hair, olive skin and huge, very dark eyes. Something about the graceful way he moved and the wary look on his face reminded her of pictures she had seen of the children of South America who made their home among the vines and orchids and broad-leaved trees of the tropical forest.

The old man with the handlebar moustache now spoke. 'This is Hubert-Henry,' he said in a braying voice. 'As you see he was not born an English gentleman – but we mean to see that he becomes one, eh, Hubert?'

And as he dug the silent little boy in the ribs, Aunt Coral saw a look of such hatred pass over the child's face that she took a step backwards and hit her backside on the big brass gong. At which point Hubert-Henry threw back his head and laughed.

Half an hour later, they sat side by side in a large black car on the way to Hubert's school. The car was a closed limo and was the kind you hire for weddings and funerals, with a glass partition sealing

17

off the chauffeur. It was a three-hour journey to Berkshire but the driver had refused to take Hubert-Henry by himself, so Aunt Coral was to deliver him to Greymarsh Towers and hand him over to the matron. The little boy, it seemed, had tried to jump from the train and run away the last time they took him back to his boarding school.

'Are you really called Hubert-Henry?' asked Aunt Coral as they began to leave London behind.

'No.'

'What are you called?'

'Fabio.'

He had a slight accent. Spanish, perhaps? Or Portuguese?

She hoped he would say more but he sat silent and sulky. Then: 'I said I'd bash the next aunt they fobbed me off with. Bash her really hard.'

'Oh, I wouldn't do that,' said Coral. 'I've got a kick like a mule. It's the hair, you see?'

'What hair?'

'The hair on my legs. We've all got hairy legs, me and my sisters. Hair gives you strength; it says so in the Bible. Samson and all that.'

But she wasn't really thinking about what she was saying. Aunt Coral was a little bit psychic, as artistic people so often are – which means that she some-times knew things without knowing how she knew them – and now she dug into her basket, took out a pad and a piece of charcoal and began to draw.

Fabio, still sulky, turned his head away. When she had finished, she put the picture down on the seat between them. Presently she heard a little gasp. The boy had seized the paper and was devouring it with his eyes, and she saw a single tear run down his cheek.

'Is that what your home was like?' she asked gently.

Fabio nodded. 'The tree's right; it was a papaya, and the monkey . . . he was a capuchin and I tamed him. But there were three huts joined together, not just one – we lived in the end one closest to the river. The chickens were ours but the goat belonged to my uncle in the middle house. You've got the pig right, but his stomach was even bigger – it touched the ground.'

'So why did you leave, Fabio?' she asked. The homesick child was still staring at the picture she had drawn; the river, the great tree with fruit hanging from its branches and the fishing boat drawn up on the shore.

'I don't know *exactly*,' he said. But he told her what he knew and she pieced the rest together.

His father, Henry Mountjoy, had been an Englishman, rich, and the owner of a big house in the country; but he was a gambler. He got into debt and in the end he had gone off to South America to find gold.

Only of course he didn't find gold. He fell ill and Fabio's mother, who was a dancer in a nightclub, had found him half starving in Rio, and had nursed him, and after a while he married her.

But he'd ruined his health and he couldn't get work and soon after Fabio was born he went back to England. Since then Fabio had lived first with his mother in Rio and then, when she moved in with another man, upriver in the forest with his grand-parents and his uncle and his cousins. There were a lot

19

of people in the three huts and very little money but Fabio had been perfectly happy. His grandfather was an Amorian Indian and knew everything, and his grandmother had worked as a cook for a Portuguese planter and had told the most marvellous stories.

Then just over a year ago his mother had come with an Englishman in a silly suit who kept mopping his face all the time and wrinkled up his nose when he passed the pig. It turned out that Fabio's father had died and on his deathbed had begged his parents, the old Mountjoys, to bring Fabio to England and bring him up as an English gentleman.

That was the beginning of the nightmare. His mother had insisted that he went. Henry Mountjoy had talked so much about his grand house in England that she wanted her son to have his share. But the grand house had been sold to pay Henry's debts, and Henry's parents took one look at the wild little boy and shuddered.

Since the grandparents were too old to turn Fabio into an English gentleman, this odd thing was to be done in a boarding school. But boarding schools, according to the old Mountjoys, had gone soft. They had tried two from which Fabio had returned much as before, only speaking better English.

Greymarsh Towers, though, was different. The headmaster believed not just in cold baths and stiff upper lips but in all sorts of things that one would have thought didn't happen any more, and the boys were vile.

'They call me "monkey" or "chopsticks" and try to tie me up. But I'm going to kill them this time. I'm going to kill them and I'm going to kill the headmaster and they can take me to prison and I don't care!'

But before he could get round to killing the headmaster, Fabio started being sick.

He was sick outside Slough, and on the far side of Maidenhead and in the entrance of a house called The Laurels in Reading, and the closer they got to Greymarsh Towers, the sicker Fabio became.

And when she saw Greymarsh Towers, Coral thought that she too would be sick if she had to return there. It was a huge bleak house with iron bars across the windows, and the stone walls looked slimy and cold.

It was now time to act. The chauffeur was supposed to drop them at the school and she was to make her own way back by train.

'Will you please wait here, Fabio,' she said to the boy. 'Keep an eye on him, Mr Fowler. Don't let him run away.'

The boy, who had begun to trust her, cowered back in his seat and Coral marched up to the front door. The smell of Greymarsh would have been enough to put her off for life. Hospital disinfectant, tortured cabbage, lavatories . . .

As for Matron, as she came out of her office she would have made a very good camel: the nose was right, the sneering upper lip, and the distrustful muddy eyes. Except that camels can't help their expressions and people can.

'I am afraid I have bad news about Hubert-Henry Mountjoy,' said Aunt Coral. 'He has been laid low with a bad attack of Burry-Burry fever and can't come back to school at present.'

Matron pursed her mouth.

'Well, of course, that is what you expect from foreign children – he probably picked it up in his hut in the jungle.'

Since Aunt Coral had just invented Burry-Burry fever she only nodded and said she would let Matron know as soon as the boy was better. She then returned to the car and said, 'I am sorry to tell you that there has been an outbreak of meningitis in the school. Everyone is in quarantine and Hubert can't go back at present.'

The little boy, who had been hunched against the cushions, now sat up and smiled. He had a very nice smile and Aunt Coral made up her mind.

'Well, I can't take him back,' said the surly driver. 'I'm going on to another job down in the West Country and I haven't a minute to waste.'

'That's all right,' said Coral. 'Just take us to the station. We'll make our own way back to London.'

Sitting on the station platform, Coral noticed the exact moment when Fabio's happiness at the thought of escaping school changed to misery at the thought of going back to his grandparents' dungeon of a house.

She hadn't had any real doubts but now she was certain. Should she use chloroform? Or the sleeping powder that Etta used?

Either way, thought Coral, Fabio was the one.

Etta and Coral had been right. Aunt Myrtle should never have been allowed to come on the kidnapping job. Almost as soon as she arrived in London she was so homesick that she thought she would die. She missed the sound of the waves on the rocks and the scent of the clover and the way the clouds raced across the high clean sky. But most of all she missed Herbert. She was used to sitting on the point every day and playing the cello to him, and now she began to worry in case he was missing her too.

Or *not* missing her, which would have been even worse.

So by the time she was sent to take Lambert Sprott to the zoo because his father was doing business in New York and his mother was buying clothes in Paris, Aunt Myrtle was in a bad way. Her hair kept falling down, she had a headache, and the map of the zoo looked complicated.

As for Lambert, he was a boy it was not easy to take to. He had pale distrustful eyes, a tight mouth, and carried a wallet full of money, a pocket calculator and his own mobile telephone so that he looked like a shrunken bank manager, except that bank managers have learnt to be friendly and Lambert had not.

All the same she was determined to do her best, and to share with the boy the beauty of the animals they saw: the knock-kneed giraffes with their long black tongues, the dignified orang-utans with the tufts of red hair under their armpits, the Mississippi alligator, smiling as he steamed in his pool.

'Oh how fascinating animals are, are they not, Lambert!' she cried, getting carried away. 'Look at those bonteboks – the way they carry their heads. And over there, the dear dik-diks – so small but so fast when they run.'

Lambert yawned. 'They smell,' he said.

Myrtle was shocked. 'Well, they have their own

scent, yes, but so do you. To a bontebok you would smell of human.'

'No, I wouldn't.'

Aunt Myrtle sighed, but she was determined not to give up. There must be a flicker of life somewhere in the boy. And there was: when something cost a lot of money Lambert became quite alert. He told Myrtle that you could get twenty thousand pounds for the horn of the white rhino, and that the Siberian tiger could fetch double that because it was so rare.

'And so beautiful,' cried Myrtle. 'Look at the markings on its throat.'

Lambert yawned again – he was not at all interested in things being beautiful and he stopped to dial a friend on his mobile telephone, but the friend was out. 'I wouldn't mind going shopping,' he said. 'I've got my own account at Harrods.'

But Myrtle had not been told to take him shopping and, ignoring his whining, she led the way across a little stone bridge and stopped dead.

They had come to the seals. The females lay about like old armchairs, coughing and grunting, but there was one, a young bull seal, who seemed to be staring directly at her.

Tears of homesickness came into Myrtle's eyes; it could have been Herbert's brother lying there! 'Oh, Lambert,' she said making a last attempt, 'look at the way his whiskers curve, and the shine on his skin. Did you ever see anything so lovely?'

'They aren't worth anything,' said Lambert in a bored voice. 'You can't get any money for seals. They're common.'

And then he opened his mouth and yawned once

more. He yawned so that Myrtle saw his unhealthy tongue, his tonsils, even the little flap of skin at the back of the throat that stops the food going down the wrong way – and something snapped inside her.

She wouldn't kidnap this loathsome child in a hundred years. The thought of waking up on the Island and knowing he was there made her blood run cold, and she could no more soil her cello case by stuffing the repulsive brat into it than she could fly. She would take Lambert back to his house and tell her sisters that she was a failure as a kidnapper, and she would go home.

Once she had decided this she felt better, but there was a long afternoon to get through still; one of the longest of her life, it seemed to Myrtle. Lambert lived in a large house bristling with burglar alarms and fitted with ankle-deep carpets, a private bar, a swimming pool, and a kitchen full of gadgets which hummed and pulsed and throbbed and which she had no idea how to use.

What Lambert's house didn't have in it was any people. His father was busy getting rich, and his mother was busy spending the money he made, so neither of them spent much time at home. Myrtle had been told to wait till the woman who gave Lambert his supper came, and hand him over.

Lambert sat down in front of an enormous telly and started zapping channels in a bored way, and Myrtle made her way to the bathroom to freshen up. She had decided to flush the chloroform down the loo; it bothered her having it when she had given up as a kidnapper, so she took the bottle and her bag of hairpins and made her way upstairs.

'What have you got there?' Lambert's suspicious voice made her turn round. He had put his telephone in his pocket and was glaring at her, narrowing his eyes. 'You're stealing something. What's in that bottle?'

He leant forward to try and snatch the bottle. Aunt Myrtle put it behind her back but Lambert kicked her hard in the shins, twisted her free arm and grabbed the bottle. Then he undid the stopper and put his nose to it.

'Don't!' cried Myrtle. 'Put it down, Lambert.'

But it was too late. The loathsome boy lay felled and quite unconscious on the floor.

Chapter Three

Minette woke up in a strange bed with a lumpy mattress and brass knobs. She was in a big room; shabby, with a threadbare carpet and faded wallpaper covered in a pattern of parrots and swirling leaves. The curtains breathed slightly in the open windows. A high mewing noise came from outside.

Then she remembered what had happened and at once she was very frightened indeed.

She had been eating a sandwich, sitting opposite a strange fierce aunt who was supposed to be taking her to her father; and suddenly the compartment started going round and round and the face of the aunt came closer and then further away . . . and then nothing more. Blackness.

She had been drugged and kidnapped, she was sure of that. She could remember the way the dreadful aunt had peered at her as if she was looking into her soul. Minette knew all about fear but now she was more afraid than she had ever been. What dreadful fate lay in wait for her? Would they cut off her ear and send it to her parents – or starve her till she did what they wanted?

And what *did* they want? Kidnapping was about getting money out of people and neither her mother nor her father was rich.

Moving in the bed, she found she was not tied up,

but the windows would be barred and the door locked.

Pushing aside the bedclothes, she walked over to the window. She was wearing her own nightdress; the aunt must have kidnapped her suitcase as well. The window was open and as Minette looked out she gasped with surprise.

For she was looking at a most incredible view. Down below her was green, sheep-cropped turf studded with daisies and eyebright. A large goose with black legs walked across it, followed by six goslings with their necks stretched out. Beyond the turf the ground sloped to a bay of perfect white sand – and then came the sea.

Minette looked and looked and looked. The sea in the morning light was like a crystal mirror; she could hear the waves turning over quietly on the beach. There were three black rocks guarding the bay and on them she could make out the dark round heads of seals. White birds circled and mewed and the air smelled of seaweed and shellfish and wind. It smelled of the sea!

'Oh, it's beautiful,' she whispered.

But of course she would not be allowed to go outside. Kidnapped children were kept in dark cupboards and blindfolded. Any minute now someone would come and deal with her. She looked round the room. Old furniture, patchwork rugs, and by the bed – and this was odd – a nightlight. She had begged and begged for one at home but neither her father nor her mother had ever let her have one.

A small snuffling sound made her turn quickly. It

had come from behind a screen covered in cutouts of animals in the corner of the room.

A fierce dog to guard her? But the noise had not been at all a fierce one.

Her heart pounding, she tiptoed to the screen and looked round it. On a camp bed lay a boy of about her own age. He had very dark hair and sticking-out ears and he was just waking up.

'Who are you?' he asked, staring at her with big round eyes.

'I'm Minette. And I think I've been kidnapped by an aunt.'

The boy sat up. 'Me too.' He blinked. 'Yes, I'm sure. I was supposed to be going back to my grandparents. She gave me a hamburger.'

'Mine gave me a cheese and tomato sandwich.'

The boy got out of bed and stretched. He too was wearing his own pyjamas. 'We'll have to try and escape,' he said. 'We'll have to.'

'Yes. Only I think we're on an island. Come and look.'

She didn't know why, but she had had the feeling at once that the sea wasn't just in front of them but all around.

'Wow!' Fabio too was struck by the view. 'What a place.'

Minette had gone over to the door. 'Look, it isn't locked!'

'I'm going out,' said the boy. 'They don't seem to have taken our clothes away. They're crummy kidnappers.'

'Unless it's all a trap.' She thought of the films she had seen – holes suddenly opening in the ground with man-eating piranhas or sharks. 'Do you think they've kidnapped us to feed us to something?'

He shrugged. 'You'd think they'd choose fatter children than us. Come on, get dressed. I'm going out.'

There was no one in the corridor; there was no one on the stairs.

Then, from behind a door across the hallway, they heard a scream, followed by a thump, and then a second scream. Someone in there was being tortured – and it sounded like a child.

Minette leant back against the wall, white-faced and trembling.

'Come on – quick!' Fabio clutched her arm.

The children ran out across the turf, over the dunes, along the perfect crescent of sand. The tide was out; it was a shell beach; there were Venus shells and cowries and green stones polished like emeralds. No one stopped them; there was no one to be seen. It would have been like Paradise except for that ghastly scream.

'Look,' said Fabio.

A group of seals had swum towards the shore and were looking at them, swimming in a semicircle, snorting and blowing . . . With their round heads they looked like a group of Russian dolls.

The children were silent, looking at the seals, and the seals stared back at them. Then suddenly they turned and swam back into the deep water.

All except one, a bull seal with white markings on the throat, who came close to the shore, and closer, till he was in the shallows with his flippers resting in the sand.

'It's as if he's trying to tell us something.'

'He's got incredible eyes,' said Minette dreamily. 'He doesn't look like a seal at all. He looks as though inside he's a person.'

'Well, seals are persons. Everything that's alive is a person really.'

But that wasn't what she'd meant.

They took off their shoes and walked on the firm wet sand between the tidemarks towards a cliff covered with nesting kittiwakes and puffins and terns. The tide was still going out, leaving behind its treasures: pieces of driftwood as smooth as velvet, crimson crab shells, bleached cuttlefish bones, whiter than snow. There was no sign of any ship. They might have been alone in the universe.

'What's that noise?' asked Fabio, stopping suddenly.

A deep and mournful sound, a kind of honking, had come from somewhere inland.

'It must be a foghorn,' said Minette.

But there wasn't any fog, nor any lighthouse to give warning if there had been.

They listened for a few moments but the sound did not come again, and they ran on along the shore. It was a marvellous island; it seemed to have everything. To their left was a green hill; two hills, actually, with a dip between, the slopes covered with bracken and gorse. The far shore would be wilder, exposed to the wind.

'If we climbed up there we could see exactly where we are. There might be other islands or a causeway. If we're going to escape we're going to have to know,' said Minette.

They had to get away – that terrible scream still rang in their ears – but Minette couldn't help thinking of where she would be if she hadn't been kidnapped. In her father's dark sitting room trying to get interested in a book till he came back from the university.

Fabio seemed to be having the same sort of thoughts. 'I can't help wondering if my grand-parents will pay the ransom for me. They're horribly mean and they don't like me.'

Minette tried to think if her parents liked her enough to pay a lot of money to get her back but when she thought about her parents her stomach always started to lurch about so she said, 'There's a little path there to the top of the hill.'

They began to run towards the gap in the dunes, forgetting the lives they had left behind, forgetting even that awful tortured scream. The wind was in their backs; it was like flying. No one could imagine anything dangerous or dark.

And then it happened! From behind the hummock of sand that had hidden them, there arose suddenly the cruel figures of two enormous women.

It was the evil aunts!

The sinister kidnappers glared at the children, and the children, terrified, stared back. Here was the tall bony aunt with her fierce eyes who had drugged Minette's sandwich, and here was the plump mad person with her scarves flying in the wind who had given sleeping powders to a defenceless boy.

The children reached for each other's hands. Minette was shaking so much she could hardly

32

stand. What punishment would they be given for escaping from their room?

It was the tall bony aunt, Etta, who spoke. 'You're late for breakfast,' she said in her fierce and booming voice.

The children continued to stare.

'Breakfast,' the other one went on. 'You've heard of that? We have it at seven and the cook gets ratty if he's kept waiting. Go and wash your hands first – the bathroom's at the top of the stairs.'

The children ran off, completely puzzled by this way of kidnapping people, and Etta and Coral followed. They were talking about Myrtle, who hadn't stopped crying since she came back.

'She's got to stop blaming herself,' said Coral. 'Mistakes can happen to anyone.'

'Yes. Mind you, Lambert is quite a mistake!'

Breakfast was laid in the dining room, a big room with shabby leather chairs, which faced the patch of green turf and the bay. All the windows in the L-shaped farmhouse had at least a glimpse of the sea. Even the bathroom, with its huge claw-footed bath and ancient geyser, looked out on the ledge of rock where the seals hauled out of the water to rest.

'Porridge or cereal?' asked Aunt Etta, as the children came in.

Minette blinked at her. 'Cereal,' she managed to say.

'Porridge,' said Fabio.

'Please,' said Etta briskly, picking up the ladle. 'Porridge, *please*.'

Fabio was the first to shake himself awake. 'This is a very odd kidnap,' he said crossly. 'And I won't eat anything drugged.'

Aunt Etta leant forward, scooped a spoonful of porridge from his plate and gulped it down.

'Satisfied?' she said.

Fabio waited to see if she yawned or became dopey. Then he began to eat. The porridge was delicious.

They were both on second helpings when the screams began again. This time they were even worse than before and were followed by sobs and wails and a low shuddering moan. Then the door opened and a woman they had never seen before ran into the room. She had long, reddish-grey hair down her back; a bloody scratch ran along one cheek and she seemed to be quite beside herself.

The children shrank back in their chairs, their fear returning. The woman looked every inch a torturer.

'Really, Myrtle,' said Aunt Etta, 'I've told the children they mustn't be late for breakfast and now look at you.'

But no one could be cross with Myrtle for long, not even her bossy sister. The scratch on Myrtle's cheek had begun to bleed again, there were tooth marks on her wrist, and though she took a helping of porridge she was quite unable to swallow it.

And when she was introduced to Minette and Fabio, her tears began to flow again.

'Yours are so nice,' she sobbed. 'They look so intelligent and friendly.'

'That's as maybe,' said Etta. 'We haven't tried them out yet.' She frowned as more bangs and thumps came from across the corridor. 'He can't stay in the broom cupboard, Myrtle. What would happen if he goes for the Hoover? We'd never get the place cleaned up again.'

'It's just for now,' said Myrtle. 'I gave him my bedroom when he first came round but I was afraid for the ducklings.'

Myrtle often had motherless ducklings keeping warm in her bed and her underclothes drawer.

'I suppose we shall have to *un*kidnap him,' said Coral. 'But how? No one's going to pay a ransom for Lambert Sprott.'

'We could offer to *give* his father some money if he'll take Lambert away,' suggested Myrtle, blowing her nose.

'Don't be silly, Myrtle,' said Etta. 'For one thing we haven't got any money – and for another he'd tell everyone about the Island and photographers would come, and journalists.' She shuddered. Keeping the position of the Island secret was the most important thing of all.

'We could turn him round and round till he was completely giddy and leave him in a telephone kiosk somewhere on the mainland,' said Coral. But she did not sound very convinced by her idea.

Myrtle began to sob again. 'I should have left him on the floor,' she gulped. 'I should never have brought him. But it seemed so cruel just to leave him there unconscious.'

'Hush. What's done is done.'

But Myrtle couldn't be consoled. 'And my cello case smells of the awful child,' she wailed. 'He puts terrible stuff on his hair.'

'Perhaps he'll settle down when we've got some breakfast into him.'

Judging by the screams and thumps coming from across the corridor though, this did not seem likely.

But Fabio was getting impatient. 'What about *us*? Are you going to unkidnap us?'

The aunts stared at him. 'Are you mad?' said Etta. 'After all the trouble we took. In any case, you haven't been kidnapped exactly. You've been *chosen*.'

Minette and Fabio stared. 'How?' asked Minette.

'What do you mean?' enquired Fabio.

Aunt Coral put down her coffee cup. 'It's time we explained. But first you'd better come and meet Daddy. He gets upset when things are kept from him.'

Captain Harper was a hundred and three years old and spent most of the day in bed looking at the Island through his telescope.

He was very deaf and very grumpy and what he saw through the window didn't please him. When he was young there had been far more geese coming from Greenland – hundreds and thousands of geese – and their feet had been yellower and their bottoms more feathery than the geese who came nowadays. The sheep had been fleecier when he was a boy and the flowers in the grass had been brighter and the seals on the rocks ten times larger and fatter.

'Huge, they were,' Captain Harper would say, throwing out his arms. 'Great big cow seals with big bosoms and eyes like cartwheels, and look at them now!'

No one liked to say that it was probably because he couldn't see or hear too well that things had changed, and when he told the same stories for the hundredth time, his daughters just smiled and tip-toed out of the room because they were fond of him and knew that being old is difficult.

'Here are the children, Father,' yelled Coral. 'The ones that have come to stay with us.'

The old man put down his telescope and stared at them.

'They're too small,' he said. 'They won't be a mite of use. You need ones with muscles. When I was their age I had muscles like footballs.'

He put out a skinny arm and flexed his biceps, and they could see a bump like a very small pea come up on his arm. 'We were all strong in those days. There was a boy in my class who could lift the teacher's desk with one hand. Freddie Boyle he was called. He was the one who put the grass snake down the teacher's trouser leg.'

The aunts let him tell the story about the grass snake and the teacher's trouser leg because it was a short one, but when he began on the one about Freddie Boyle's brother, who'd run over his own false teeth in a milk float, they shepherded the children out quietly.

'He won't notice,' they said.

When they went downstairs again they found Art, the cook, wiping porridge off his trouser leg. He had tried to give Lambert some breakfast and had it thrown in his face.

'Nasty little perisher you've got in there,' he said. 'Best drown him, I'd say. Shouldn't think his parents would want him back.'

Before he escaped and was washed up on the Island, Art had worked in the prison kitchens, which was why he made such good porridge. Because he'd killed a man once, Art didn't like the sight of blood and it was always the aunts who had to chop the

37

heads off the fish before they went into the frying pan or get the chickens ready for the pot. Another thing Art didn't like to do was anything energetic.

'I don't know my own strength,' he would say, when there was anything messy or difficult to be done. 'I might forget myself and do someone an injury.'

This didn't seem likely – Art was a skinny person who hardly came up to Aunt Etta's shoulder – but he'd quickly locked the door on Lambert and, leaving him to scream for his mobile telephone, retreated to his kitchen.

But Aunt Etta and Aunt Coral now led the children into the garden behind the house. It was time to explain.

The garden was surrounded by grey walls to give shelter from the wind; but no walls on the Island were built so high that they shut out the view of the sea. Aunt Myrtle had gone down to play her cello to the seals. A bumblebee droned on a clump of thrift. It was very peaceful.

'Perhaps I'd better tell you a story,' said Etta. 'It's a true story and it begins with five girls coming to an island with their widowed father to look for a new life.

'They found a lovely and deserted place, but ruined, abandoned. All the people who had lived there had left long, long ago. Even the ghost in the old graveyard seemed to have gone away.'

Minette sat with her arms hugging her knees and her eyes closed. She loved stories.

'So the girls and their father repaired the house and planted a garden and learnt to fish and cut peat and do all the things the Islanders had done before they left. But of course the world outside was changing. Oil was spilled into the sea, and sewage, and trawlers started to use nets that caught even the smallest fish. The water became overheated by nuclear power stations. You'll have learnt all that at school.'

Minette nodded, but Fabio only scowled. Absolutely *nothing* useful had been taught at Greymarsh Towers.

'Soon the sisters and their father found themselves looking after things that came ashore. Oiled seabirds . . . stunned seals . . . poisoned squids . . . And other things . . .'

Etta paused and looked up at Coral who raised her eyebrows in a warning way. *Not yet*, said Coral's eyebrows. *Remember what we decided*.

Etta nodded and turned back to the children.

'The sisters worked from dawn to dusk. One of them was an idiot; she started shaving her legs and marrying tax inspectors, so she was no good . . . And one went off to foreign parts to stop people eating rare animals. And the others got older and became aunts . . .

'And then one day they realized they might die before long – they might become extinct – and then what would happen to all the creatures? So they decided to find people to carry on after them. Sensible people. Young ones. People who knew how to work.'

There was a long pause. Then:

'Us?' said Fabio shyly.

Both aunts nodded.

'Yes,' said Aunt Etta. 'You.'

39

Chapter Four

So Fabio and Minette were set to work.

It was the hardest work they had ever done and it didn't stop from morning to night.

The day began with fifty press-ups on the grass behind the house. Etta was in charge of these, rising up and down on her elbows with her skirt tucked into her navy-blue knickers. She had thirty-one pairs of these, one for each day of the month. The children had seen seven of them on the washing line and she explained that it made it easier having things the same colour and the same shape so that one didn't have to think about things which didn't matter – like which of one's knickers were which.

Then they began on the chores. The aunts ran a smallholding; there were six goats and a cow, and two dozen chickens whose eggs needed to be collected, and fresh straw which needed to be put down.

There were buckets of mash to be taken to the eider ducklings whose mother had been fouled in a fishing net, and two seal pups who had to be hand-fed from a bottle. The children had thought feeding the seals might be fun, but it wasn't. The pups prodded and squealed when the milk didn't come fast enough; it was like being bashed into by two blubbery tanks.

A puffin with a splint on his leg lived behind the house, and in a tin bath with a wooden lid was an octopus with eye trouble.

And as they worked, the children were watched – *tested*, you could say – because anyone who was disgusted by a living thing, however odd, was no use on the island.

Minette was marched down to the strand by Aunt Etta and shown a pile of pink and purple slime.

'These are stranded jellyfish,' said Etta. 'Put them back into the water. You'd better wear these.'

She handed Minette a pair of rubber gloves and stood over her while she carried the wobbling blobs back into the sea.

Fabio was taken to a big tank in the paddock and told to pick up an eel with a skin disease.

'Hold him behind the head while I scrub,' Coral ordered him. 'He's got scabies.'

When they were in bed at night, the children tried to think how to run away. Fabio now slept in a box room next to Minette and with the door open they could talk.

'We can't stay here and turn into slaves,' said Fabio.

'No. Except the aunts are slaves too. They work harder than us.'

This was true, but Fabio said it made no difference. 'We'll have to steal a boat.'

But their beds were warm; they had nightlights; the sea sighed softly beneath their open windows – and, before Minette could see even the smallest tiger on the ceiling, they were both asleep.

And while they slept the aunts discussed them.

'Well, so far so good,' said Etta. 'They haven't squealed or squirmed or wriggled. Yet. Or said "Ugh!" I can't bear people who say "Ugh!" '

'And they seem to be keeping to the rules,' said Coral.

The rules had been set out on the first day.

'You're not to go near the de-oiling shed in the cove,' Etta had said. 'Nor up to the top of the hill.'

'Nor to the loch between the hills.'

The children had grumbled about this.

'It's exactly like that fairy story about Bluebeard's Castle,' said Minette. 'You know . . . if you open the seventh door you'll have your head chopped off.'

But they had obeyed – even Fabio who had been so difficult to control in his grandparents' house. Nothing, though, could stop Fabio asking questions.

'What's that honking one hears sometimes? It sounds like a foghorn.'

'If it sounds like a foghorn I expect it *is* a foghorn,' said Etta, and that was the end of that.

But what of Lambert?

Lambert went on screaming and kicking and wailing for his mobile telephone and Art (who did not know his own strength) just put down his tray and ran for it whenever he brought him his food. They had locked him in a room above the boathouse; it had been the Captain's study and the doors and windows were strong.

At mealtimes they tried to decide what to do with him. Coral thought they might set him adrift in a dinghy with enough food for a few days, and Fabio thought he should be dipped in boiling oil. But they never got very far because whenever they talked about Lambert, Aunt Myrtle always began to cry because she blamed herself for having kidnapped such an awful boy and brought him to the Island.

Then, on the fourth day, as they came down to breakfast, Fabio and Minette found all the aunts looking at them with a pleased expression. Their teachers at school had looked like that when they had passed an exam.

'Your work has been satisfactory,' said Etta.

'And your conduct,' said Coral, flicking her beads out of the sugar bowl.

'So we have decided that you may work in the de-oiling shed today.'

The children thought this was an odd kind of reward for being good; de-oiling seabirds is about the messiest job there is. But they kept quiet and presently they were following Aunt Etta along the cliff path and down to the cove on the far side of the bay.

The de-oiling shed was a wooden building set back into the cliff. At high tide the water came almost to the walls but now they could reach it by scrambling over low rocks covered in seaweed, and pools full of anemones and shrimps and tiny scuttling crabs. The children would have liked to linger and explore but Aunt Etta thrust them forward and knocked loudly on the door.

'Are you decent?' she called.

The children looked at each other. How could sea birds *not* be decent?

There was a scuttling noise, followed by a plopping sound – and then the door was opened from the inside.

The children had expected rough wooden walls; shelves, perhaps; a slatted floor. But the shed was more like the inside of a Turkish bath.

There were tiles on the walls; water gushed from a tap into a large, blue-painted sink decorated with seashells and into two tubs set under the high windows. Hairbrushes lay on a low table, and hand mirrors, and there were more mirrors on the wall.

But it was what was inside the sink or lying on the wet floor which held them speechless. You can read about such things as often as you like but seeing them is very different.

There were four mermaids in the shed. They wore knitted tops which Myrtle had made but their tails of course were free – no one would have worn one of Myrtle's knitted tops on their tails – and when she saw that the children, though pale, were not going to make a fuss, Aunt Etta introduced them.

'This is Ursula,' she said, leading them up to a very old lady who sat in the sink nearest the door. Her hair was full of broken pieces of shell and sticks; the egg case of a dogfish hung over one ear and she had only one tooth – a long one which came down over her lower lip.

But the girls who shared one of the tubs under the window were young. They were twins but they were not at all alike. Queenie was very pretty with golden ropes of hair and a pert look in her bright blue eyes; but Oona's hair was dark with a green sheen on it and her grey eyes were sad.

And, sprawled on the floor, trying to hide a piece of gum she had been chewing, was the girls' mother, Loreen. She was a fattish, blowzy person and looked as if she had given up on life. The knitted top she'd hastily put on was crooked and the flowers in her hair were very dead.

Aunt Etta frowned at the chewing gum, which Loreen had cadged from Art. 'A disgusting habit,' she said, glaring at the packet.

'It's my nerves,' said Loreen. 'I've got to have something for my nerves, with the state I'm in.'

She was certainly in a state. As well as a bruise on her cheek and a black eye, Loreen was very badly oiled. All of them were oiled but Loreen was really covered in the stuff.

'Have you been taking your tonic?' Etta asked.

'We've all been taking it. But we're not better. Oona's ears are still bad and Queenie's itching all over. We can't go home yet,' said Loreen firmly. 'Not for a long time.'

Etta ignored this. The way absolutely nobody wanted to go away even when they were healed was beginning to annoy her.

'They're not very big,' complained the old crone, staring at Fabio and Minette. Everyone knew about the children and that they had been chosen and not kidnapped.

'We're strong though,' said Fabio, who was getting tired of this.

But there was one other person still to meet. In a washing-up bowl on the floor floated something pale and smooth which turned out to be a baby.

But not any baby. Probably the fattest baby in the universe. His wrists were lost in layers and layers of fat; his neck was covered by a whole waterfall of chins; his small blue eyes were sunk in his swollen

45

cheeks like currants in a pudding and he was bald.

'My youngest,' said Loreen. She looked tired rather than proud. 'His name's Walter.'

The children did not know what to say. Walter looked more like an overgrown maggot than a merbaby – but he was not oiled! When the oil slick came his mother had held him aloft and now Aunt Etta turned away from the washing-up bowl with pursed lips because Walter was exactly the kind of spoiled, pampered male of whom she particularly disapproved.

'Right,' she said to the children. 'Time to start work. The detergent's in that bottle – it gets diluted with three parts of water. And when you've finished put them under the hose – all of them. Oona gets three of these drops in each ear and remember, with anything fishy, scrub in the same direction as the scales or you'll be in trouble.'

The door closed behind her, and Queenie, the pretty pert twin, pulled a face.

'What's the matter with you?' she said cheekily. 'Cat got your tongue?'

'Now, Queenie,' said her mother wearily. 'Maybe they've never seen mermaids before.'

'As a matter of fact we haven't,' said Minette.

She picked up the roughest of the scrubbing brushes while Fabio poured out the detergent. Then they walked over to Queenie's sink, picked up her tail and began to scrub.

The mermaids had not had an easy time even before they were caught in the oil slick. Loreen's husband was a bully – mermen are often bad-tempered – and the bruise on her cheek came from him.

Then a bad thing happened to Oona, the younger of the twins. She was caught in a fishing net and dragged aboard a fishing boat, but the person who unwrapped her wasn't an ordinary sensible fisherman; it was a chinless wonder called Lord Terence Brasenott who thought catching a mermaid was a terribly good joke.

'I say, what jolly fun,' he kept saying. 'What a pretty little thing. I'll take you back with me,' he'd said and pawed her with his horrible hands and tried to kiss her.

Oona spent three days in his cabin, weeping piteously, and by the time she managed to free herself and dive overboard her voice had completely gone. This happens sometimes when people have a serious shock; it is bad for anyone, but for mermaids, who are famous for singing, it is particularly bad. Even now, Oona could only manage a whisper or a croak.

No sooner had they got over this disaster than a French mermaid turned up from Calais and started making eyes at Loreen's husband. French mermaids have two tails and the whole thing went to the silly man's head and he turned his wife and children out of their cave and set up home with his new love. He even turned out his grandmother, Old Ursula, which was particularly hard on Loreen as she had to take her along. Being lumbered with your own grandmother can be difficult but when it's your husband's grandmother it can seem seriously unfair.

What happened next was Queenie's fault. She was

pretty and she was headstrong and though everyone had warned her what ships were like nowadays, she insisted on sitting on a rock and singing to the captain of a cargo boat coming from the Middle East.

'Arabia's in the Middle East,' she said, 'so they'll be carrying gold and treasure like in the Arabian Nights; you'll see.'

Queenie had a good voice and she'd kept up to date with tunes and didn't waste time on 'Hey Nonny No' sort of songs, and it so happened that the captain was musical and a little drunk and when he heard her he got very excited and ran his ship on to the rocks.

But what came spilling out were not doubloons and pieces of silver which might have made the mermaids rich. What came out . . . was oil. Masses of thick, black, greasy oil straight from the oil wells of Saudi Arabia. It caught the whole family fair and square, half blinding them, weighing down their limbs. They just managed to reach the safety of the Island and land wearily on the shore – and there the aunts had found them.

The children learnt all this while they cleaned them up. It was incredibly hard work. The girls' tails were slippery and surprisingly heavy – and Queenie was ticklish so when they began to scrub she started giggling and thrashing about. By the time Aunt Etta returned, the children were soaked through and dirty and tired but she took no notice at all. They had to swill down the floor of the hut, and then the mermaids' tails were wrapped in clingfilm so they could be put into wheelbarrows and taken down to the bay without them drying out. Only Old

Ursula stayed where she was and admitted that though the children might be small, they knew how to work.

When they had finished in the mermaid shed, the children were taken to the house for a drink of fruit juice and a biscuit, and then they were sent to help Aunt Coral clean out the chicken house. Fabio's family had kept chickens in South America so he knew what to do, and he and Coral had an interesting conversation about the tango, which she was fond of dancing under the light of the moon.

'You don't happen to know the steps?' she asked him.

Fabio looked doubtful. 'I watched my mother when she danced in the cabaret.'

'Good,' said Aunt Coral. 'I've always wanted a partner.'

Fabio was not at all sure that he wanted to dance the tango with a very large aunt who had stuffed him in a tin trunk and kidnapped him. But he was too polite to refuse and he had noticed the night before that the moon was far from full so that he could only hope she would forget.

Then in the afternoon things got strange again because Aunt Myrtle took them down to the point to meet the seals.

They lay about by the edge of the water, the cows dozing while they waited for their pups to be born, the bulls jostling each other and shoving to test their strength.

But one seal was sitting quite alone on a rock. He had turned his back on the rough games of the other seals and was staring romantically out to sea. It was the seal who had come close to the shore on the first day; they would have known him anywhere.

'Herbert, I'd like you to meet Fabio and Minette,' said Myrtle, just as if she was introducing someone in a drawing room.

Herbert opened his eyes very wide and looked at them. It was an extraordinary look for a seal; both children stepped back a pace; they felt as though they had been weighed up and examined by a great intelligence.

'He can't be an ordinary seal,' said Fabio.

Aunt Myrtle looked at him gratefully. 'No, dear, you're absolutely right. Herbert *is* a seal but he's a very special kind of seal. He's a selkie.'

'What's a selkie?' asked Fabio.

Myrtle sighed. 'It's not easy to explain,' she said, 'because it's all to do with legends and beliefs. There aren't a lot of *facts*.'

'Tell us,' begged Minette.

Aunt Myrtle sat down on an outcrop of rock and the children came to sit beside her.

'All sorts of things are told about selkies,' she began. 'That they are the souls of drowned men . . . that they are a kind of faery and if someone sticks a knife in them they will turn back into humans.'

'A *knife*!' Minette was horrified. 'How could anyone do a thing like that?'

Aunt Myrtle shrugged. 'I certainly couldn't.' But she blushed, thinking of how she had sometimes wondered what would happen if she did get up the courage. Would Herbert really turn into a man, and if so, what *kind* of a man? Might he become a showing-off kind of man like a bullfighter, always trailing his cape about? Or a really boring person who thought about nothing except making money?

Herbert had come to the Island many years ago. His mother had brought him because he had a cough which wouldn't get better and it had got about that the Island was safe even for seals who were not well. The aunts had healed his cough and then Myrtle had played the cello to him and he had stayed.

They had known of course that he wasn't an ordinary seal. Herbert did not speak exactly, but he understood human speech and sometimes when he and his mother talked together in the selkie language, which is halfway between human speech and the language of the seals, Myrtle could make out . . . not the words exactly, but the sense of what they said.

'He had a very famous grandmother,' said Myrtle, dropping her voice. 'At least, we think she was his grandmother. She was called the Selkie of Rossay and there are stories told about her all over the islands.'

'Tell us,' begged Minette again. She could never get enough stories.

So Aunt Myrtle pushed her hair out of her eyes and began.

'The Selkie of Rossay was a female seal who lived about a hundred years ago. One night she came out of the sea and shed her sealskin and danced with nothing on by the light of the moon and a fisherman came and fell passionately in love with her.' Myrtle paused and gave a wistful sigh. 'You know how it is,' she said, 'when people are dancing by the light of the moon.'

The children nodded politely though they didn't really.

'So he hid her sealskin and brought her some clothes and married her and she stayed with him and had seven children and they were perfectly happy. Though when they sat down, even on dry days and in completely dry clothes, the children left a damp patch. Not . . . you know . . . anything to do with nappies. Nothing nasty – it was an absolutely *fresh* damp patch – but it showed they had seal blood.'

Herbert was listening most intently. He moved closer, he cleared his throat.

'Then one day when she was rummaging in a trunk, the selkie found her old sealskin and she put it on and the sea called to her – it called to her so strongly there was nothing she could do – and she dived back into the sea and after a while she married a seal and had seven seal children. But for the rest of her life she was in a terrible muddle, calling her sea children by the names of her land children and her land children by the names of her sea children and never really knowing where she belonged. At least, that is the story.'

Myrtle stopped and Herbert gave an enormous sigh and rolled over on to his side. He might have forgotten how to speak like a human, but he had understood every word and the story Myrtle told was his own.

The Selkie of Rossay *had* been his grandmother. She had gone crazy in the end from not knowing whether it was better to be a woman or a seal, and Herbert's mother, the youngest of her seal children, had stayed with her till she died, seeing that she didn't starve even when her teeth fell out and her eyes filmed over.

Herbert's mother was still alive; she came ashore sometimes and nudged her son and tried to get him to make up his mind about what he wanted to be because she knew it didn't matter whether one was a man or a seal so long as one stuck to it.

But Herbert took after his grandmother. He couldn't decide. When Myrtle played the cello to him it seemed that being human was the best that he could hope for. But when he watched Art and saw what he would have to do if he was a man – wear trousers with braces or zips, and shoelaces and all that kind of thing – he would dive back into the water and turn over and over in the waves and think: This is my world; it is here that I belong.

When the children got back to the house, they found Art with a large piece of sticking plaster on his forehead. He had tried to give Lambert some lunch and Lambert had torn the plate out of his hand and hurled it across the room. Then he'd lain down on the floor and drummed his heels and screamed for his father and his mobile telephone.

'I'd have thumped him,' said Art now, 'but I daren't. I don't know my own strength. I might have pulped him into a jelly.'

Fabio didn't say anything but he was beginning to wonder about Art's great strength. Meanwhile Lambert was still in the room above the boathouse.

'But he can't stay there,' said Coral. 'The boy is a fiend. We've *got* to get rid of him.'

But though they discussed it for the rest of the day,

53

none of the aunts could see how this could be done short of killing the child – which they would very much have liked to do, but which was not the kind of thing that happened on the Island.

Chapter Five

When the children came down to breakfast the next day they saw at once that the aunts were worried. Etta's moustache stood out dark against her pale face and her nose had sharpened to something you could have used to cut cheese.

'I really don't want to operate,' they heard her say, 'but it's serious. She's completely egg-bound.'

'Who's egg-bound?' asked Fabio.

Aunt Etta ignored him.

'I've tried massage; I've tried Vaseline; I've tried a steam kettle,' she said to her sisters.

'What about castor oil?' suggested Coral.

'It's worth a try, I suppose.'

'Can we help?' asked Minette.

'No.' Etta looked up briefly. 'Well, perhaps you can carry the buckets. We're going up the hill. And kindly fold your napkins properly when you leave the table. You left them in a disgusting heap yesterday.'

It was quite a procession which wound its way up the hill. Etta carried an enormous bottle of castor oil, Fabio lugged a footstool and a primus stove, Minette had two buckets and a bundle of rags.

The path was steep and the morning was warm but Aunt Etta kept up a fierce pace. She also chose to give them a lecture as she went.

'Now I want to make it *absolutely* clear to you that I will *not* have favourites on this island. The unusual creatures you will be working with are *no more important* than the ordinary ones. A sick water flea needs help just as much as a mermaid. A flounder is *exactly* as important as a selkie. I hope you understand this because if you don't, you're not going to be any use doing your job.'

The children said, yes, they had understood it, but when they reached the top of the hill they were pleased they had been warned.

There were two hills, actually, with a dip in between which held a loch of dark, peaty water. On the far side of the loch was a great pile of brushwood and boulders and bracken. It looked like one of the stockades that the settlers in America used to build to protect themselves from the Indians.

But what stuck out over the top of the stockade was not an American settler. It was the head of an absolutely enormous bird.

The head was black but its beak was a bright yellow and made the children think of those great machines – crunchers or diggers or shovellers – that one sees looming over building sites. Its eyes were yellow too, huge and round and mad-looking, and as they stared they were blasted backwards by the deep honking noise they had heard on the first day.

'What is it?' stammered Fabio.

'It's a boobrie,' said Aunt Etta, striding round the edge of the loch. 'And I can tell you there aren't many of those left in the world. They're a sort of cousin of the dodo – people thought they were extinct but they weren't. They developed on a different island and the sailors didn't find them so they just grew and grew and grew. But then people started doing atomic tests and that kind of nonsense and the ones that were left managed to fly away.'

She led them round the other side of the stockade and they saw a short ladder propped against the side of the nest. Aunt Etta climbed up it and beckoned to the children to follow but they hung back, thinking of the huge yellow eyes, the dreadful beak.

'Hurry up!' said Etta and, as they still hesitated, she turned round, took a deep breath, and let them have it. 'I have to tell you that kidnapping you was quite the most unpleasant experience any of us have had: that boarding house full of yacking women, and the London Underground with all those fumes. If you think we'd have gone to all that trouble just to let you get eaten by some bird, you need to have your heads examined. Anyway boobries are vegetarians, at least this kind are – more's the pity.'

So the children followed her up the ladder and jumped down into the nest which was trampled flat and lined with moss and feathers.

The boobrie was not really *so* enormous. She was smaller than an African elephant – more the size of an Indian one. It took a lot of courage to look up at her but when they did the children stopped being afraid. She *could* hurt you, of course, by stepping on your feet for example, but they could see that she was a bird with serious troubles of her own.

The nest was ready for eggs but there were no eggs to be seen. The boobrie's chest looked sadly naked so that they knew it was her own feathers she had plucked out to make a warm lining, but a lining for what? Where were the eggs and where the chicks that would follow?

'I have to tell you that I am very worried about her,' said Aunt Etta. 'Being egg-bound is a most serious business.'

'You mean her eggs are stuck inside her? She can't get them out?' asked Minette.

'That's right. And she's too uncomfortable to go and look for something to eat.'

'Doesn't she have a mate to bring her food?' asked Fabio.

Aunt Etta snorted. 'She had but she's lost him.'

'You mean he's dead?'

'He may be, for all I know. Or he may have lost the way or forgotten all about her. You know what men are.'

This annoyed Fabio. 'I'm a man, or I will be, and I'll never leave my wife to starve in a nest. Never.'

'Why did you say it's a pity she's a vegetarian?' Minette wanted to know.

'Because it makes it hard for us to feed her. We could have thrown her a frozen side of beef, but to dredge up all those sludgy sea lettuces and sea noodles and gutweeds takes hours,' said Etta. She was stamping round the boobrie, batting her with a stick, thumping her. 'Get up, you stupid bird. I'm trying to help you.'

At first the boobrie wouldn't move; she sat hunched and shivering and from her throat came a single squawk which seemed to be her way of saying 'Ow!' But Etta was merciless. She thumped and scolded and prodded the bird till she struggled to her feet and stood there swaying and honking.

Then she climbed on to the footstool and peered into the boobrie's back end and there, sure enough, was a glimmer of white speckled with blue.

'You can make seventy-two omelettes from one boobrie's egg,' said Etta when the children had had a look.

But of course she didn't want seventy-two omelettes – she didn't care for omelettes anyway – she wanted living chicks. 'The next part is going to be messy,' she warned.

But the children stayed to help, dipping rags into the hot castor oil and handing them to her as she dabbed and swabbed at the opening.

'We'll just have to wait and see,' she said when she'd finished. 'But if this doesn't work . . .'

'Could she . . . die . . . ?' asked Minette in a quavery voice.

'Anyone can die,' said Etta snubbingly. 'Including you and me.'

But before she marched the children down again she took them up the further hill, which was the highest point of the Island.

The view was incredible. To the west, miles and miles of unbroken water with the sun making a golden path between the clouds, and to the east, a long way off but with their outlines sharp and clear, two islands; one hilly, one low and long.

And on a grassy ledge overhanging the wild northern shore was an ancient burial ground, with leaning and broken gravestones covered in lichen and battered by the rain.

'There's supposed to be a ghost here,' said Etta. 'But she only turns up every hundred years or so.'

'What sort of a ghost?'

'A *good* ghost. A kind of hermit. She was called Ethelgonda and she lived on the Island and looked after the creatures.'

'Like you,' said Minette.

'Not in the least like me,' said Aunt Etta crushingly.

'I didn't think good people became ghosts,' said Fabio.

'Well, a spirit then.'

The children spent the rest of the day collecting the special seaweeds that the boobrie ate and barrowing them up to her nest. Each time they watched anxiously for a sign of an egg but nothing seemed to be happening at all.

They were getting ready for bed that night when Myrtle came upstairs excitedly, her long hair flying.

'Come down for a minute,' she said. 'Herbert's mother has come and she wants to meet you.'

She hurried them down to the rocks and there, sure enough, sitting beside Herbert was a smaller seal, a cow with the same whitish mark on her throat as her son. Herbert's mother was old – there was something weary about the way she held her head – but she lumbered up to them, and snorted in a very welcoming way, while her son looked on proudly.

'This is a great honour, you know,' said Myrtle, hopping about like a young girl. 'She doesn't come out of the water often now; it tires her to be on land. Herbert will have told her about you.'

Since it is difficult to shake hands with a seal, they bowed their heads politely, and Herbert's mother came closer and said something, speaking in a low voice and in the selkie language. The children thought she was asking them to help Herbert make up his mind about whether to be a person or a seal and, when they were back in their rooms, Fabio had an idea. 'We could just cut him with a knife. Not hard. Just a nick – then he'd become human and that would be that.'

'Oh, we couldn't!'

'I don't see why not. Then Myrtle would have a friend. He could learn the piano and they could play duets.'

But when he thought about it, Fabio knew that Minette was right. He couldn't make even the smallest nick in that smooth and shining skin.

It was on the next afternoon that the children had a shock. They had taken yet another load of seaweed to the boobrie and were shovelling it into the nest when the bird gave the loudest honk they had heard yet. For a moment they thought it might be an egg, for the honk was a welcoming one.

But it wasn't. The boobrie was looking at the loch.

The children turned to follow her gaze – and gasped.

A head had appeared in the middle of the lake.

But what a head! White and smooth and enormous . . . like the front end of a gigantic worm. After the head came a neck . . . also smooth . . . also white . . . a neck divided into rings of muscle and going on and on and on. It reared and waved above the surface of the water, and still more neck appeared . . . and more and more. Except that the neck was getting fatter, it couldn't all *be* neck – the bulgier part must be the body of the worm: a worm the size of a dozen boa constrictors.

The boobrie honked once more and the children clutched each other, unable to move.

The creature was still rising up in the water, still getting longer, still pale and glistening and utterly strange. Then it turned its head towards them and opened its eyes which were just two deep holes as black as its body was white.

'Whooo,' it began to say. 'Whooo' – and with every 'oo' the air filled with such a stench of rottenness and decay and . . . *old*ness . . . that the children reeled backwards. And then it began to slither out of the water . . . it slithered and slithered and slithered and still not all of it was out of the lake – and suddenly the children had had enough. Leaving their wheelbarrows where they were, they rushed down the hill to the house and almost fell into the sitting room where the aunts were having tea.

'I didn't expect you to knock,' said Aunt Etta, putting down her cup. 'One knocks at the doors of bedrooms but not of sitting rooms when one is staying in a house. But I do expect you to come in quietly like human beings, and not like hooligans.'

But the children were too frightened to be snubbed. 'We saw a thing . . . a worm . . .'

'As long as a train . . . Well, as long as a bus.'

'All naked and white and smooth and slippery . . .'

'It said "Whoo" and came at us, and its breath . . .' Minette shuddered, just remembering. 'It came out of the lake and now it's coming after us and it'll coil round and round us and smother us and—'

'Unlikely,' said Aunt Etta. She passed the children

62

a plate of scones and told them to sit down. 'It seems to be very difficult to get you to listen,' she said. 'I'm sure that all three of us have told you how unpleasant we found the whole business of kidnapping you.'

'Yes, indeed,' said Coral. 'That loathsome matron like a camel.'

'So it is not very likely that we would go to all that trouble to feed you to a stoorworm,' said Etta.

Being safe in the drawing room, eating a scone with strawberry jam, made Fabio feel very much braver.

'What *is* a stoorworm?'

'A wingless dragon. An Icelandic one; very unusual. Once the world was full of them, but you know how it is. Dragons with wings and fiery breaths in the skies. Dragons without wings and poisonous breaths in the water. The wingless ones were called worms. You must have heard of them: the Lambton Worm, the Laidly Worm, the Stoorworm.'

But the children hadn't.

'If his breath is poisonous . . . he breathed on us quite hard,' said Minette. 'He said "Whoooo" and blew at us. Does that mean we'll be ill or die?'

Aunt Coral shook her head. 'He's only poisonous to greenfly and things like that. We use him to spray the fruit trees. And he probably wasn't saying "Whoooo", he was saying "Who?" – meaning who are you? He talks like that; very slowly because he comes from Iceland and they have more time over there.'

But Minette was still alarmed. 'Look,' she said,

staring through the window. 'Oh look, he's slithering down the hill . . . He's coming closer . . . He's coming here!'

Aunt Myrtle came to stand beside her. 'He'll be coming to visit Daddy,' she said.

'They're good friends,' explained Coral to the bewildered children. 'They think alike about the world – you know, that the old days were better.'

Standing by the open sitting room door, they watched bravely as the stoorworm slithered into the hall, slithered up the first flight of stairs, along the landing, up the second flight . . . In his bedroom they could hear the Captain shouting, 'Come along, my dear fellow, come on in,' and the front end of the worm went through into the Captain's bedroom while the back end was still in the hall trying to lift its tail over the table.

Fabio had stopped feeling frightened but he was becoming very suspicious. 'Is there anything we have to do to the stoorworm?' he asked. If the mermaids needed scrubbing and the seals had to be given a bottle four times a day, and the boobrie's food had to be wheelbarrowed up a steep hill, it seemed likely that the stoorworm too would mean hard work.

And he was quite right. 'It's a question of seeing that he doesn't get tangled up,' said Aunt Etta. 'In the water he's all right but you will see a few trees we've stripped of lower branches – those are stoorworm trees and when he's on land we help him to coil himself round them neatly, otherwise he gets into knots. It's best to think of him as a kind of rope, or the flex of a Walkman.'

Fabio didn't say anything. He had already gathered that when Aunt Etta said 'we' she meant him and Minette – and she went on to explain that the worm was a person who liked to think about important things like *Where has yesterday gone?* or *Why hasn't God made sardines without bones?*

'The trouble is he's so long that his thoughts don't easily get to the other end, and that upsets him,' said Etta. 'He wants to have an operation to make him shorter, but you must make it clear that we will *not* allow it. Plastic surgery,' said Aunt Etta, fiercely tapping her nose, 'is something we could never permit on the Island.'

'If you're bothered by his breath you can always give him a peppermint,' said Coral. 'Though why everyone in the world should smell of toothpaste is something I have never understood. And now you'd better go and fetch the barrows from the hill.'

Chapter Six

'We must start to think seriously about running away,' said Fabio sleepily.

'Yes, we must,' agreed Minette, yawning.

They had gone on saying this each night – it was almost like saying their prayers – but they hadn't got much further. It wasn't just that they would have to steal the *Peggoty* from the boathouse, they would also have to know in which direction to sail her. And of course running away has two parts to it. There is running away *from* somewhere and there is running away *to* somewhere.

'It's all right for you,' Fabio said. 'You've got two proper parents. All I've got in this country is an awful school and awful grandparents.'

'Yes.' But Minette was doubtful. If she ran away to her father, her mother would be cross and if she ran away to her mother, her father would be cross. 'I'd just like to wait till the boobrie's laid her egg.'

And in the end, before they could make further plans, the children always fell asleep.

But as the days passed there was one thing that really annoyed Fabio, and that was Lambert.

Fabio didn't mind working hard. All the same, he and Minette both had blisters on their hands from trundling the wheelbarrows up and down to the loch; Minette had strained her wrist trying to get a comb through the old mermaid's tangled hair; and both of them were bruised by the young seals bumping and flopping against them as they gave them their bottles. And there was Lambert doing nothing – absolutely nothing – except kicking and screaming and throwing his food about.

'Why doesn't someone thump him?' said Fabio crossly.

But nobody did. Aunt Myrtle wasn't a thumper and the other aunts said that using force when training animals never worked. As for Art, he might have killed a man once but that was as far as it got. So each day Lambert was brought his food on a tray and each day he kicked and yelled for his father and his mobile telephone while Fabio and Minette did his share of the chores.

It was at the end of the first week that Fabio cracked, and it was because of the stoorworm.

The children had grown very fond of the worm. He ate the peppermints they gave him without fuss and the questions he asked were interesting, like *Why don't we think with our stomachs?* or *Why are we back to front in the mirror but not upside down?*

But wrapping him round a tree was an awful job. It wasn't just his thoughts that got stuck halfway down his body, it was all the messages which told his lower end what was happening, and on a day when they had spent a whole hour disentangling him from a bramble thicket, Fabio suddenly snapped.

Art was just making his way down to the boathouse with Lambert's lunch on a tray.

'I'll take that for you, Art,' said Fabio.

Art handed over the tray and Fabio opened the door.

Lambert looked up. Then he did what he always did when someone came into the room; he picked up whatever was closest to him and threw it hard. This time it was a sawn-off log ready to go on the fire.

Fabio ducked neatly. Then he threw the tray at Lambert. The tray contained a bowl of lentil soup, a slice of bread and butter, fried tomatoes on toast and a banana milkshake. All of these landed on Lambert except for the bread and butter which went slightly wide.

'Yow! Whee! Yuk!' Lambert spluttered and danced round the room, blinded by the tomatoes which were the large splodgy kind with a great many pips.

Fabio gave him a few moments to clean himself up. Then he said, 'Right. You're not getting anything more to eat till you come and work. Minette and I are sick of doing the jobs you ought to be doing.'

'I won't! I won't come and work!' Lambert tried to stamp his foot on the floor but stamped it into his soup bowl which split in half and skidded across the room. 'I won't stay here on this horrible island and I won't stay with these creepy women and I won't do anything. I want my father and I want my mobile telephone and I want to go home.'

Fabio waited. 'I don't care what you want,' he said. 'Minette and I want things too, but that doesn't mean we get them. From now on you're going to do your share and if you don't I'm going to thump you.'

Lambert had cleaned the tomato out of his eyes

now. 'You'd better not,' he said. 'I'm bigger than you.'

This was true but it didn't bother Fabio. 'You may be bigger but you're weedier.'

Lambert was a coward, but Fabio was very small and slight. Lambert put up his fists and danced forward. He had never boxed but he had seen people do that on the telly.

Fabio on the other hand *had* boxed. He didn't care for it but it was taught at Greymarsh Towers as part of making people into English gentlemen. He let fly with his right hand and landed a blow on Lambert's chin.

'Oow! Eeh! . . . You've bust my jaw. I'm going to tell my father. My father's rich and . . . Oowee . . .' Lambert was crouching down on the floor nursing his chin and moaning.

'Get up,' said Fabio.

'I won't.'

'Yes, you will. Get up or you'll be sorry.'

Lambert got slowly to his feet. The bruise on his chin blended nicely with the colour of the tomato smeared on his collar. Then suddenly he went for Fabio, tearing at his cheeks with his fingernails.

It hurt, but to Fabio it was a relief. He knew about fighting dirty. He had been doing it ever since he was three years old in the streets of Rio and if that was what Lambert wanted it was fine with him. Ignoring the blood streaming down his cheeks, he took hold of a handful of Lambert's hair and yanked the snivelling boy's head backwards, knocking it against the wall. Then he kicked him extremely hard on the shins.

'Ow!' moaned Lambert. 'Stop it!'

'I'll stop it as soon as you say you'll come and do your share of work.'

'I don't want to. I want my father. I want my mobile tele—'

Fabio yanked his head forward, then pushed it back again hard against the wall, and went on kicking.

'Are you going to come out and work or not?'

'No.'

Fabio kicked again – and suddenly Lambert crumpled up and collapsed on the floor.

'All right,' he blubbered. 'I'll work, but stop it.'

Fabio stopped at once. 'Come on, then,' he said. 'You can help me muck out the chicken house.'

The aunts saw the boys come. Fabio was carrying the remains of Lambert's lunch on the tray, including the broken soup bowl.

'You can take it out of my pocket money,' he said, handing them the pieces.

'What pocket money?' asked Aunt Etta.

'Even kidnapped children have to have pocket money,' said Fabio firmly.

So Lambert began to work. He worked badly and he worked slowly. He complained because the television was on the blink and whenever he could, he crept off to look for his mobile telephone which he was sure Myrtle had hidden somewhere. But when he stopped for too long, Fabio just looked at him and he picked up his tools once more.

Everyone agreed that such a tiresome, blathering boy had to be kept away from the unusual creatures

– the selkies and the boobrie and the stoorworm – so they gave him jobs to do in the house or with the animals on the farm. But a couple of days after Fabio had beaten him up, Lambert crept down to the shore with a lemonade bottle he had stolen from the larder. Inside the lemonade bottle was a message he had written to his father telling him to come and rescue him, and he was going to throw the bottle into the sea.

But he never got as far as doing that. Instead he dropped the bottle, which smashed on the stones, leaving a dangerous mess of broken glass, and came back to the house blubbering and screaming at the top of his voice.

'I saw a *thing*! I saw a horrible creepy thing!' His whole body shook with terror. He looked as if he was going to have a fit.

'What sort of a thing?' asked Fabio.

He and Minette were sitting at the kitchen table, shelling peas for supper.

'A girl . . . all queer and horrible. She didn't have any legs – not any!' He sobbed and gulped again and a runnel of snot ran down his nose.

Minette handed him her handkerchief. 'What do you mean, Lambert?' she asked.

'The bottom end of her was a monster. She had a tail all covered in scales. It was growing from her body.' Lambert retched and turned his head away. 'I saw it. I *saw* it. I won't stay here, I won't!'

Minette and Fabio exchanged troubled glances.

'What was the top of her like?'

'I don't know . . . she had sort of green hair – and when I screamed she flopped her tail – I *heard* it flop . . .' He shuddered. 'And then she dived into the water.'

'It sounds like Oona,' said Minette in a low voice. 'Of course it would be her – she's been frightened enough already by that ridiculous Lord Brasenott. I'll go and comfort her. If only it had been Queenie, she'd have seen Lambert off.'

She slipped out and Fabio was left alone with the blubbering Lambert.

He had had an idea.

'Lambert,' he said. 'Listen to this, because it's important. When Minette and I first came, we saw all sorts of strange creatures – mermaids like you've seen and a long slithery worm and a giant bird – oh, all sorts of things – but then we realized they weren't real. They couldn't be real because creatures like that don't exist. I mean, there aren't any such things as mermaids, are there?'

Lambert had stopped crying. He was actually listening.

'No,' he said. 'There aren't.'

'So what has happened, Lambert, is that you're imagining them. It's like having a vision or a dream. And it's because of something that Art puts in the food. He uses a flour made of seaweed and it has a drug in it that makes you see things. He doesn't mean to harm us but it's the only kind of flour you can get here.'

'They aren't really there?' asked Lambert, sniffing the snot back into his nose. 'She wasn't there – that horrible girl and the awful tail that she flopped with – that wasn't there either?'

'No it wasn't. And anything else you see like that

72

will just be a dream. You've heard of drugs that give you visions, haven't you? They're called halluci—'

But here Fabio gave up, not sure of how to pronounce *hallucinogenic* or even if that was the word he meant. 'And it's best not to say anything to anyone – even if you think you see other things. Just don't take any notice, and if you get back to your father don't tell him, he'd only laugh at you.'

It worked. Lambert gave a few more gulps; he was still blotched, he was still hiccuping unpleasantly, but he was calm.

And from then on, if Lambert saw anything unusual he was sure it was because of something in the food.

The aunts weren't happy about Fabio telling lies, but it seemed safer than letting Lambert go screaming all over the Island and hurting the feelings of the creatures that he came upon.

And so the days passed. Minette and Fabio still talked about getting away but they always fell asleep before they could work out how to do it, and slowly the beauty of the place – the great wide skies, the flaming sunsets and the never-ending sound of the sea – seemed to be becoming a part of them.

But meanwhile in London all hell was breaking loose.

73

Chapter Seven

Eight days after Minette ate her drugged cheese and tomato sandwich, Minette's mother, Mrs Danby, rang Edinburgh to ask if Minette could stay with her father for an extra week. Minette's term had started but that was not the kind of thing that bothered Mrs Danby.

'I have the chance of a job filming in Paris,' she said.

This wasn't strictly true. What she did have was yet another boyfriend who said he'd take her to France for a bit of a 'jolly'.

Professor Danby, whom she'd interrupted as he was preparing an important lecture on 'The Use of the Semi-Colon', did not at first understand what she was saying.

'I can hardly keep Minette longer, when I haven't got her,' he said in his dry, irritable voice.

There was a pause at the other end while Mrs Danby fought down the slight fluttering in her stomach.

'Don't be silly, Philip. I sent Minette to you more than a week ago. She's been with you since the fifteenth.'

'No, you didn't. I had a telephone message to say you were keeping her with you and taking her to the seaside. I remember it quite clearly.'

The professor had in fact been rather pleased because the lecture he was giving was part of an important series – 'The Use of the Semi-Colon', 'The Use of the Comma', 'The Use of the Paragraph' and so on – and he needed to get on with his work without being bothered by a child.

Now, though, he too began to feel as though his stomach was not quite where it should have been. But of course being the sort of people they were, the Danbys immediately began to blame each other.

'You must be mad, not letting me know she hadn't arrived.'

'*I* must be mad?' hissed the professor. '*You* must be mad. Any normal mother would ring up to see that her daughter had arrived safely.'

'And any normal father would ring and find out why she wasn't being sent.'

'Are you accusing me of not being normal?' said the professor in a dangerously quiet voice. 'A woman who stubbed out her cigarette on a poached egg.'

'It wasn't a poached egg, it was a fried egg. And if you hadn't kept turning the lamps off because you were too mean to pay the electricity bill I'd have seen it wasn't an ashtray. And anyway, how a man who leaves a bath full of scum every time he—'

'Scum!' yelled the professor down the phone. 'Are you accusing *me* of leaving scum? Why I couldn't even get *into* the bath without wading through a heap of your unspeakable toenail clippings.'

They went on like this for some time but then they remembered that their only daughter was missing and pulled themselves together.

'Can she have run away?' wondered Mrs Danby.

'Why should she run away? She has two perfectly good homes.'

'Yes. But she's been looking a bit peaky. And she sees tigers on the ceiling. Perhaps I should have let her have a nightlight.'

'If every child who sees tigers on the ceiling ran away, there'd be very few children left in their homes,' said the professor.

But obviously the next thing to be done was to go to the police. So Professor Danby went to the police station in Edinburgh and Mrs Danby went to the police station in London. Then she rang her ex-husband and said that the police wanted them to come together and compare their stories exactly.

'You have to come down,' said Mrs Danby. 'And quick. They say there's no time to waste.'

So the professor took the train to London and the next day both of Minette's parents sat side by side in a taxi on the way to the Metropolitan Police Station.

The officer they saw this time was a high-ranking one, a detective chief superintendent who had a secretary sitting beside him to take everything down.

'Now, I understand that you have heard nothing since your daughter disappeared ten days ago?' he asked. 'No messages? No ransom demand?'

Both the Danbys shook their heads.

'I have very little money,' said the professor. 'I'm on the staff of the University and they pay abominably. It's a disgrace how little—'

'And I'm on the dole,' said Mrs Danby, unusually honest. 'So even if they asked us for money, it wouldn't help.'

The detective wrote this down. 'Now tell us, please, Mrs Danby, exactly where and when you last saw your daughter.'

'It was at two o'clock on the fifteenth of April. At King's Cross Station, Platform One. I handed her over to an aunt—'

'Wait a minute!' The superintendent's eyebrows drew together sharply. 'You mean *your* aunt . . . or *her* aunt . . . ?'

'No. *An* aunt. An aunt from an agency. Minette always travelled with aunts.'

The detective seemed to find this very interesting. 'Go and get me the file on the Mountjoy case,' he said to the secretary. 'Sergeant Harris has it.' He turned back to the Danbys. 'Now tell me from what agency you hired this aunt. It's an extremely important point.'

Mrs Danby frowned. 'Well, generally they came from an agency called *Useful Aunts*. I've used them for years – they're very reliable. But I think . . .' She rubbed her forehead. 'I'm not sure . . . I think this one may have been labelled *Unusual Aunts*. Yes, I think so. And there was some writing above that which said "My Name is Edna". Or maybe it was Etta.'

'If you hadn't rotted your brain with tobacco you might be able to remember,' said the professor under his breath.

But at that moment the secretary came back with a blue folder. 'Yes,' said the detective as he opened it. 'Yes. The two cases are extraordinarily similar.' He looked up at the Danbys. 'Another child disappeared on the same day as your daughter and he

77

too was put in the charge of an aunt. I think we're getting somewhere at last!'

The old Mountjoys were always pleased when Hubert-Henry went back to boarding school. They hated having children about and they could never quite forgive their son for having married a foreign dancer in a nightclub and producing such an unsuitable grandson.

Then just a week after Hubert-Henry had left for Greymarsh Towers, a letter came from the head-master which told old Mr Mountjoy that even though Hubert was not at school because of Burry-Burry fever, the full fees for the term would still have to be paid.

That did it of course. Mr Mountjoy rang the headmaster and said what nonsense was this about Burry-Burry fever and where was the boy, who had been delivered to school on the first day of term?

And the headmaster said, no he hadn't, the aunt from the agency had told Matron that Hubert-Henry was ill.

So after the old Mountjoys had shouted down the telephone and threatened to sue the headmaster they went to the police. They might not be fond of Hubert-Henry but he was their grandson and their property and if anyone had taken him they wanted to know the reason why.

Which meant the police knew of two cases in which a child had vanished in the care of an aunt and it was now that the Great London Aunt Hunt began.

The police only knew about two aunts because Lambert's father was still in America, so that the boy had not yet been reported missing. But two aunts were enough to be going on with – and the newspapers and the police and the general public now went slightly mad.

Aunt Plague Menaces the City screamed the headlines, and *Monster Aunts on Killer Spree!*

Once people had been warned they saw these murdering women everywhere.

An aunt was caught outside a supermarket trying to impale a sweet little baby with a giant knitting needle while his mother shopped inside.

'I was only trying to spear a wasp,' she quavered, 'I didn't want it to sting the child.' But she was hauled off to the police station and it was only when they found the back end of the squashed insect in her knitting bag that she was set free.

An even more sinister aunt was seen in Hyde Park, kicking in the head of a little boy who lay in the grass.

'I seen her clear as daylight,' said a fat man who'd been walking his dog and sent for the police. 'Kicking like a maniac she was!'

And, 'Look how he's crying, the poor little fellow,' said the other dog owners who had crowded round – and it was true that the boy, holding on to his football, *was* crying. Anyone would cry, seeing their aunt bundled into a police van when she'd been showing them how to curl a penalty into the top right hand corner of the goal. She'd been a striker for the Wolverhampton Under-Eighteens and he thought the world of her.

There was talk in Parliament of a curfew for aunts, forcing them to be in bed by eight o'clock; the *Daily*

79

Echo said aunts should be electronically tagged like prisoners – and an elderly lady was arrested in the shoe department of a department store for abusing her great-niece who was trying on shoes for a party.

'She was shouting and screaming at the child and her eyes were wild,' said the woman who had turned her in – and the aunt would probably have gone to prison, but while she was in the cells, the shop assistants downed tools and marched on the police station with banners, demanding that she should be freed.

'I wouldn't just have shouted at the girl, I'd have wrung her neck,' said a motherly shop assistant to the reporters standing round.

'The poisonous child had thirty-nine pairs of shoes out and she was throwing them round the floor,' said another shop girl. 'If you ask me, that aunt had the patience of a saint not to scream at her earlier.'

So the police let her go and then the newspapers said they were too soft and aunts should be flogged like in the good old days.

Meanwhile posters of Etta and Coral were stuck up in police stations and public libraries and bus shelters everywhere. These pictures had been drawn by an artist from the descriptions he had been given by the people who had seen them last, and they were extremely odd. Aunt Etta had a nose like a pickaxe, a blob of hair like a jelly bag on top of her head and a moustache she could have twirled, it was so big. Aunt Coral had a mad squint in one eye, seven pairs of earrings in each ear and absolutely no neck.

Have you seen these women? it said at the bottom of the posters.

But of course no one had, because women like that do not exist. And so the days passed and still the police had no clues to go on. The Aunts' Agency had closed down and it seemed as though the stolen children and their kidnappers had vanished off the face of the earth.

Chapter Eight

Aunt Etta woke and stretched and immediately felt very strange. Something had happened. And the something was important: perhaps the most important thing that had ever happened to her.

She got out of bed and went to the window. Her long grey pigtail hung down her back; her hairy legs and bony feet stuck out from under her flannel nightdress, but her mud-coloured eyes were as excited as a young girl's.

Yet there was nothing unusual to be seen. A flock of gulls were out fishing; the sun was just beginning to come up behind the two islands to the east.

'All the same, there is something,' thought Aunt Etta, and the excitement grew in her. 'Only what?'

Then she realized that the excitement was coming from her feet. It was being sent through her toe bones, and up her ankle bones and through her body.

For a moment she felt quite faint. Could it be . . . ? But no . . . that would be a miracle; she had done nothing to deserve anything as tremendous as that.

The sound of heavy breathing made her turn. It was Coral. She too was in her nightdress, folds of it wrapped round her like a bell tent, she too was barefoot and she too was panting with excitement.

'Oh, Etta,' she gasped. 'I feel so strange.'

Coral's long hair, which she dyed an interesting

gold, hung down her back; she looked like a mad goddess. 'I feel as though . . . only it can't be, can it? Not after a hundred years?'

'No . . . it can't.'

But they clutched each other's hands, because it hadn't stopped, the extraordinary, amazing . . . feeling.

'We must wake Myrtle. She's musical.'

But there was no need to wake Myrtle. Myrtle did not wear a nightdress; she wore pyjamas because she often went out before dawn to talk to the seals and she thought that pyjamas were more respectable. They were made of grey flannel so that she did not show up too much in the dusk and for a moment her sisters did not see her lying on the floor with her face pressed to the threadbare carpet.

'Myrtle, do you feel—' her sisters began.

But before she could answer, Myrtle lifted her head. They had never seen their sister look like that.

'Can it be?' began Coral.

'We must go up the hill,' said Myrtle and she spoke like someone in a dream. 'We must turn our faces to the north.'

'But dressed,' said Etta, coming to her senses for a moment. 'Not in our nightclothes. Not even if—'

But her sisters took no notice and Etta herself only had time to put on her dressing gown before there was a thumping noise from next door. It was the Captain's walking stick banging on the wall and it meant, 'Come at once.'

The sisters looked at each other anxiously. If he had heard it too it could strain his heart. So much excitement is bad for old people.

And when they first saw the Captain they were very worried. He was lying slumped on his pillows, his eyes shut, and he was trembling so much that the whole bed shook. But when they came up to him, they were amazed. Captain Harper was a hundred and three years old, but he looked for a moment like a boy.

'I've heard it,' he murmured. 'I've heard it and I've felt it. Even if that's all, even if there's no more than that, I'll die happy now.'

'We're going on to the hill, Father,' said Etta. 'We'll tell you as soon as—'

The door burst open and Fabio and Minette came running into the room. They had tumbled straight out of bed, bewildered and still half asleep, and followed the sound of voices.

'Something's happened,' said Minette. She was wearing quite the silliest nightdress that even her mother could have bought, covered in patterns of dancing elephants and picnicking zebras, but with her dark hair wild about her shoulders and her bewildered eyes, she seemed to be listening to music from another land. 'We were woken . . .'

'It's a feeling . . . only it isn't only a feeling.' Fabio shook his head, trying to understand. 'It's a sound, except it's all through us. We're not making it up.'

The three aunts and the old Captain looked at the children, and nodded. It was a pleased nod, and it meant that the children were all right; they were proper ones, without a touch of a Boo-Boo or a Little One. Lambert, they were sure, would have heard and felt nothing.

'You'd better come with us. Get your shoes on at least.'

Outside the feeling was stronger. Minette and Fabio, struggling for words to describe it, were lost. They followed the aunts on to the turf path which led to the hill. Minette wore Myrtle's shawl round her shoulders – no one had taken time to dress properly.

The 'feeling', whatever it was, was growing stronger. It came through the soles of their feet, but also now from above, from everywhere. If they'd been doubtful whether it meant anything, the creatures would have put them right at once. In the dawn light the birds wheeled round the cliff in a frenzy of agitation. The seals, usually drowsing on the point at this hour, were all in the water, swimming towards the northern strand – and in the lead was Herbert. Like all selkies he slept with one eye open: he had been the first to know that something incredibly important was going to happen and at once he had put aside his everyday worries. What did it matter now whether one was a man or a seal? He moved through the waves like a torpedo – and close behind Herbert came his mother.

The sky was changing. It was filled with strange colours which belonged neither to the dawn nor to the sunset; colours that the children had never seen and afterwards could not describe.

On her great nest, the boobrie honked with all her power . . . honked and stirred . . . and flapped her wings, trying to fly off after the others, but she couldn't, with the eggs so heavy and stuck inside her

. . . and she pushed her muscles together, pressing and pressing as she tried to become airborne . . .

The stoorworm came out of the lake and slithered over the ground, following the aunts and the children. He was no longer the muddled creature who had lost control of his far end. He moved like a great serpent, controlled and lean and fast.

Down by the house the goats butted their horns against the walls of their sty, and broke free and went galloping along the shore like mad creatures.

The door of the mermaid shed opened and Loreen and her daughters slithered across the rocks and plunged into the water.

'To the north,' she shouted, holding Walter in the crook of her arm, and they set off for the wild strand beneath the hill.

'Wait for me, wait for me,' shouted Old Ursula, but they had gone and she was left beating her tail furiously against the side of the sink.

The Sybil had come out of her cave. The mucky old prophetess was not talking about the weather now. She was writhing and moaning, her face had turned blue and her hair was standing on end. 'It's going to happen,' she said. 'It's going to happen.'

But the aunts did not wait for her to tell them what. They raced panting up the hill with the children beside them, and all the time the feeling was getting stronger, was going through every cell in their bodies.

They reached the top of the hill – and then they were certain. From all sides it came now, like the breath of the universe. Below them the sea boiled against the northern shore; the mermaids, their troubles forgotten, trod water and stared towards the horizon; the seals made a semicircle, and those who were more than seals, who had been human once, could be seen bowing their heads.

And to make everything certain, from behind the largest of the tombstones with its strange carvings, there now rose a white, mysterious wraith, with rays of light coming from her face, and outstretched hands.

'It's Ethelgonda,' breathed Aunt Etta, 'Ethelgonda the Good!' And everyone fell to their knees, for this was a ghost who had not appeared for well over a hundred years.

The saintly hermit was smiling. She was totally happy; she enfolded them in her blessing.

'Yes,' she said, in a deep and beautiful voice. 'You have not been mistaken. What you have heard is most truly the Great Hum.'

Minette and Fabio, who had been spellbound by the apparition, heard the sound of the most heartfelt sobbing beside them and turned their heads. All three of the aunts were crying. Tears streamed down Aunt Etta's bony cheeks, tears made a path through Aunt Coral's nourishing night cream, tears dropped on to Aunt Myrtle's hands as she brought them to her face.

'It is the Hum,' repeated Aunt Etta, in a choking voice.

'It is the Hum,' nodded Aunt Coral.

And Myrtle too said, 'It is the Hum.'

'What is—' began Fabio but Minette frowned him down. She felt that this was not the moment for questions.

'So does that mean . . . ?' faltered Aunt Etta, and the children looked at her, amazed. They did not know that this fierce woman could sound so shy and uncertain and humble.

The hermit nodded. 'Yes, my dears,' she said in her melodious voice. 'It means that this place above all others has been chosen. You have been blessed.'

The aunts rose slowly to their feet. They could still not quite believe what they had heard, yet the Hum now was everywhere, filling the sky, coming up from the earth.

'So *he* is really coming? After a hundred years?'

The holy woman nodded.

The aunts did not ask *when* he was coming. They knew that one must not pry into mysteries, but accept them gratefully, and they were right.

'I can say no more,' said the saint. 'You must hold yourself in readiness.'

And then she vanished and they were left alone with their miracle.

'You heard what Ethelgonda said. We must hold ourselves in readiness. Readiness means cleaning. Readiness means tidying. Readiness means cooking and scrubbing and fettling. It always has and it always will,' said Aunt Etta.

She was almost her old brisk bossy self as she sent the children to scour out the goat sty and swill down the floor of the mermaid shed and pick up the litter washed ashore.

Almost, but not quite. None of the aunts were quite the same. Etta still hung her navy-blue knickers on the line each morning, but sometimes she patted her bun of hair like a young girl invited to a party. Coral's clothes got wilder and wilder; she was painting a great underwater mural on the back of the house in all the colours of the rainbow, and the tunes that Myrtle played on her cello had become very powerful and loud.

'If only Dorothy was here,' said Etta, who missed her sister badly. Hitting people on the head with their own woks was nothing to the excitement of what was to come.

The Captain insisted on clean pyjamas every day so that he would not be caught short, and the old Sybil danced about in her cave in a frenzy of excitement. She still thought it was unwise to wash her face and hands but she decided bravely to wash her feet. This took a long time (mould had grown between her toes and mould can be interesting – the blue-green colours, the unusual shapes) but once one has heard the Great Hum life is never the same.

The creatures, in their own way, were as excited, and now the aunts understood why it had been so difficult to get anyone to go away. They must have known that something special was going to happen, even if they did not know exactly what.

Even the animals that never talked; even the herrings and the haddock and the flounders . . . even the lugworms buried in the sand seemed to be excited.

'How can a lugworm be excited?' Minette wanted to know, but when Aunt Etta dug one up for her, she saw that it might be so.

As for Art, he baked buns – hundreds and

hundreds of buns which overflowed his cake tins and had to be stored in sealed bin bags in the larder. But the buns he baked were not ordinary buns, and nor were the omelettes they had for lunch and tea and supper ordinary omelettes.

Because something very wonderful had happened out there on the hill after Ethelgonda vanished. They were turning to go home when they heard a sound from the boobrie's nest which stopped them in their tracks.

It wasn't the mournful honking they were used to: it was a proud and cheerful clucking – a noise full of motherhood and joy. Pressing and pressing her muscles together to try and follow the others had not made the boobrie airborne, but it had done something else. And there it was; an enormous, blue-spotted and totally egg-shaped egg!

But the most touching thing happened the next day when they went up to congratulate the bird once more. For the egg she had laid when the Great Hum went through her body and she had pressed so hard, had been followed by three more. Four gigantic spotted eggs had rolled together and were keeping warm beneath her body, but when she saw the aunts and the children the boobrie moved aside, examined each egg very carefully – and then pushed one out towards them with her great yellow foot.

'Be careful, dear,' said Myrtle. 'It mustn't get cold.'

With difficulty, for the egg was heavier than a cannonball, they rolled it back . . . and the boobrie pushed it out again with her enormous foot.

The same thing was repeated three times – and then they understood.

'It's a present,' said Minette, awed. 'She wants us to have it.'

Minette was right. The boobrie wanted to *share*. There was nothing to be done except to fetch Art and load the egg on to a barrow – and since seventy-two omelettes are an awful lot of omelettes, the great bun bake began.

It was hard for the children to be patient during those days of waiting. They knew that when the time came they would find out what the Great Hum meant and who was coming. But on a day when Fabio was sent out for the third time to make sure that not so much as half a cigarette carton or a cotton reel had been washed up on the north shore, he dug in his heels.

'I think you should tell us,' he said. 'Me and Minette, I mean. We can keep secrets.'

'We will tell you when the time is ripe,' said Aunt Etta, and they had to be content with that.

But what had been happening to Lambert?

The aunts were right. Lambert had slept through the beginning of the Hum and heard nothing.

When he did wake up at last, he realized that the house was empty. Doors stood open; there was no sign of Art in the kitchen. Everyone, though Lambert did not know it, was out on the hill.

'I want my breakfast,' said Lambert crossly, but there was no one to hear him.

By the time he was dressed he did hear a kind of thrumming noise, but to Lambert the magical sound seemed to be the kind of noise a generator might make, or some underground machinery.

But he was interested in the open bedroom doors. Since he had begun to work, Lambert had been allowed to come back into the house to sleep, but Myrtle and the others kept him firmly out of their rooms. Myrtle had not forgotten how he had frightened the ducklings when he first came.

Now, though, Myrtle's door stood open. Her bed was unmade and the ducklings had grown enough to manage out of doors.

Lambert crept in. His shifty eyes took in all Myrtle's little treasures and he sneered. Fancy bothering to pick up bits of driftwood and veined pebbles and arranging them on the bookcase as though they were ornaments. There wasn't a single thing in her room, as far as he could see, that was worth tuppence.

Then he stopped dead. Propped against the corner of the room was Myrtle's cello case. The cello wasn't inside it; he could see it leaning against another wall, half covered with a shawl, so the case would be empty.

Lambert crept closer. He knew he had been carried away in it though he could remember nothing. He had overheard Myrtle talking about it to her sisters.

And that meant that anything he had been holding when he was snatched might still be there!

Lambert's face was flushed with excitement, his thin lips were parted. If only the case wasn't locked!

And it wasn't! He tried the clasp, and it opened easily. The inside of the case was lined with blue velvet, faded and torn in places because it was so old.

At first there seemed to be nothing there except a crumpled silk scarf and a spare bow. Then as Lambert groped about in the back of the case, his hand found something dark and small which had been covered by the cloth.

Lambert's fingers closed round it with a cry. He had found it. He had found his mobile telephone!

He would get away now! He was safe. Hiding the telephone under his shirt, Lambert went back to his room and pulled the chest of drawers across the door. Then he crouched down like an animal with its prey and began to dial.

Three days after Lambert found his telephone, the children woke shortly after midnight to find Aunt Coral and Aunt Etta standing by their beds.

Fabio was so sleepy that he thought at first it was the full moon and he was expected to dance the tango with Aunt Coral, but it wasn't that.

'Put some clothes on,' said Aunt Etta. 'And clean your teeth.'

'We cleaned them before we went to bed,' said Minette.

'Well, clean them again. No one with gunge on their molars is worthy to hear what we have to tell.'

Still half asleep, the children stumbled up the hill after the two aunts. At the top they found Aunt Myrtle sitting over a fire she had made, ringed by stones, and it was by the flicker of the flames and to the sound of the sea sighing against the rocks below that the children learnt what they wanted to know.

'Mind you, what I'm going to say won't mean much to you unless you know your history, and I doubt if you know a lot of that,' said Aunt Etta. 'So let me start by asking you a question. What does the word *kraken* mean to you?'

Fabio was silent but Minette said shyly, 'Is it a sea monster? A very big one?'

Etta nodded. 'Yes. It is a sea monster, and it is bigger than anything you can imagine. But it has nothing to do with all the silly stories you hear. Nothing to do with rubbish about Giant Blobs or outsize cuttlefish or octopuses that pull people down to the ocean bed. No, the kraken is . . . or was . . . the Soul of the Sea. It is the greatest force for good the ocean has ever known.'

Fabio and Minette looked at her surprised. This wasn't at all the way that Aunt Etta usually spoke.

So then she began to tell them the kraken's story. It took a long time to tell and the fire had burnt down and been rekindled many times before it was finished, but the children scarcely stirred.

'There was a time when everyone in the world knew about the kraken,' Aunt Etta began. 'They knew about his huge size and that when he rested, and his back was humped out of the water, he was taken for an island. They knew that when he reared up suddenly, the sea churned and boiled and no ship that was near him had the slightest hope of avoiding shipwreck.

'But they knew too that for all his size, the kraken was a gentle creature. His eyes were full of soul and when he opened his mouth one could see that instead of teeth he had rows and rows of tendrils which were the greeny-gold colour of a mermaid's hair. Through this forest of tendrils, the sea poured in, and it was the sea which nourished him: the tiny invisible creatures which make up plankton were all that the kraken needed for food.

'They knew that the kraken came from the Far North and that the language he spoke best was Polar, though he understood other languages also. But mostly the kraken did not speak. The kraken sang. Or perhaps singing is not quite the right word. What the kraken did was to hum. It was a deep, slow sound and it was like no other sound in the world, for what the kraken hummed was the Song of the Sea. It was a healing song. If you like, it was the Breath of the Universe. Whales can hum too and Buddhist monks who spend their lives on high mountains trying to understand God . . . and small children when they are happy – but the sound they make is nothing compared to the sound made by the kraken.

'For many years the kraken swam quietly round the oceans of the world humming his hum and singing his song and stopping sometimes to rest. And when he stopped, people who did not know much said: goodness, surely there wasn't an island out in that bay before, but people who were wise and in touch with the things that mattered, smiled and felt honoured and proud. Because when the kraken came, they remembered what a splendid thing the sea was: so clean and beautiful when it was calm, so mighty and exciting and awe-inspiring when it was rough. It was as though the great creature was guarding the sea for them, or even as though somehow he was showing them what a treasure house it was.

Look! the kraken seemed to be saying. *Behold . . . the sea!*

'In those days the kraken made it his business to circle the oceans of the world each year and whenever he appeared, people started to behave themselves. Fishermen stopped catching more fish than they needed and threw the little ones back into the sea, and people who were dumping their rubbish into the water thought better of it, seeing the kraken's large and wondrous eyes fixed on them. And when he went on again it was to leave the sea – and indeed the world – a better place.

'It was like a blessing, to have seen the kraken,' said Aunt Etta now. 'It brought you luck for the rest of your life.'

'Did you ever see him?' asked Minette.

Aunt Etta shook her head. She looked very sad. 'No one living now has seen him. He hasn't been seen for a hundred years or more. He was dreadfully hurt once and he went into hiding.'

The hurt that was done to the kraken was not to his body. The skin of a kraken is a metre deep and no other animal can threaten him. No animal would want to – he travelled with a whole company of sharks and stingrays and killer whales who would have died rather than harm him.

But human beings are different. They always have been: interfering and bossy and mad for power. No one knew what kind of whaling boat had shot a harpoon into the kraken's throat. Was it a Japanese ship or one belonging to the British or the Danes? Did the whalers mistake the kraken for a humpback whale, or were they just terrified, seeing a dark shape bigger than anything they had ever seen rear up in front of them?

Whatever the reason, they let off the biggest of their harpoons and hit the kraken with terrible force in the softest part of his throat.

The kraken probably didn't believe it at first. No one had ever tried to harm him. Then he felt the pain and saw the dark dollops of his blood staining the sea.

When he understood what had happened, he began to thrash about, trying to rid himself of the harpoon – and the rope snapped. But the pain was still there and the kraken reared up, trying to dislodge the hooked horror in his neck. As he did so, the tidal wave made by his body tossed the whaling boat up, and drew it under the sea, and every one of the men was drowned, which was as well because the sea creatures who had travelled with the kraken would have torn them limb from limb.

And the kraken swam away to the north, the harpoon still in his throat. The pain died away and presently an old sea nymph came with her brood of children and cut the hook out of the kraken's flesh with razor shells and soon there was only a small scar left to show where it had been.

But the scar in the kraken's soul remained. He had travelled the world to sing the Song of the Sea and to heal the people who lived by it – and they had stabbed him in the throat. The kraken was two thousand years old, which is not old for a kraken, but now he felt tired. Let human beings look after themselves! He swam still further north, and further still to where the wildness of the sea and the large number of humped islands made him invisible, and he turned his back on the world, and slept.

And while he slept, people forgot that there had been such a creature, and the stories about him got wilder and wilder until this healing monster was jumbled up in people's minds with Giant Blobs and vicious triffids and nonsense like that.

And the sea got muckier and muckier and more and more neglected.

But of course everyone did not forget. The sea creatures remembered – the seals and the selkies, the mermaids and the nixies, and the people who lived and worked on the islands and by the shore.

And the aunts remembered.

'Oh yes, we always remembered,' said Etta now. 'Our father told us about him and our grandfather told our father. We have always known, but we never dreamt—'

She fell silent, overcome by her feelings and the children gazed into the embers of the fire and thought about what they had heard.

Why am I not frightened, Minette wondered. Once she would have been terrified at the thought of a great sea monster swimming towards them, but now she felt only wonder. And something else: a longing to help and serve this creature she had never seen. She felt she would do anything for the kraken when he came. Which was silly, because how could an ordinary girl do anything for the mightiest monster in the world? But she didn't feel silly. She felt awed and uplifted as though some amazing task awaited her.

Fabio didn't feel quite like that. Fabio felt that the

98

story he had heard needed a celebration. So he did
something rather noble. He turned to Coral, sitting
in her cloak beside him, and said:

'Aunt Coral, the moon is full – or very nearly.
Would you like to dance the tango?'

Chapter Nine

Stanley Sprott, Lambert's father, had had a good time in America. He had bought three factories and a cinema and turned out a family living in a house next to the cinema so that he could bulldoze it and build a Fast Food restaurant. There had been a court case and a fuss because the family had a disabled child and a sick mother, but Mr Sprott had won. He always did win because he knew how to hire the best lawyers and now, as the chauffeur drove him in his Mercedes from the airport, he reckoned that his trip to the States would earn him a clear million dollars.

Beside him in the car sat his bodyguard, Des, a large man with small eyes and an even smaller brain. Des had only learned to read when he was 25 and he liked to show that he could do it, so as they stopped for the traffic lights he looked at the posters on the wall of the police station and said: 'There's some mad aunts been on the rampage, kidnapping children. They're offering a thousand pounds reward if anyone's got any info.'

Mr Sprott thought this was very funny.

'Aunts!' he snorted as the car moved on, leaving the pictures of Aunt Coral and Aunt Etta flapping in the breeze. 'Trust the police to be fooled by a bunch of aunts!'

Mr Sprott had a very low opinion of the police, who had tried to interfere with some of his enterprises and been thoroughly foiled.

Arriving in his house, he stood for a moment in the hallway and looked about him. He had the feeling that somebody who should have been in his house, was not.

But who? Who was it that was not there? While Des went to turn off the burglar alarms and look for letter bombs, Mr Sprott thought about this.

Well, for one thing his wife was not there. But there was nothing strange about that. His wife had faxed him from Paris to say she was going to go and buy some more clothes in Rome, and she had faxed him from Rome to say she was going to buy some more clothes in Madrid.

So it wasn't Josette Sprott who should have been there and wasn't, and it wasn't the housekeeper who always had two hours off in the afternoon.

Which meant that it was his son, Lambert.

'Lambert!' bellowed Mr Sprott, standing in the middle of the hallway.

No answer.

'Get him on the intercom,' Mr Sprott told Des.

But though all the rooms were connected electronically, Lambert did not appear.

Mr Sprott was not alarmed, but he was surprised. He had told Lambert when he was coming back and the boy, though an awful sniveller, was fond of his father.

Mr Sprott went to his study, sent out for a secretary, and was soon deep in his business affairs.

But when the housekeeper came back in the early

evening, Mr Sprott was reminded of his son once more.

'Didn't you bring Lambert, sir?' she asked him. Her voice was hopeful. She really hated the boy.

'How could I bring Lambert? I haven't got him. I never had him – he's staying here with you.'

'No, he isn't. There was a message saying he was joining you in America. It was left by the aunt – she said there'd been a call.'

'The aunt? What aunt?'

'The aunt from the agency. She took Lambert to the zoo and when I got back the boy was gone.'

The flapping posters, the notice of the reward, ran through Mr Sprott's mind. They didn't seem so funny now.

'I'm sorry, sir, but—'

'Be quiet.' Mr Sprott was scowling. 'I'm going to the police. Tell Merton to bring the car round.'

But at that moment, very faintly, a telephone rang upstairs.

It was his personal phone, or rather one of them. Mr Sprott bought mobiles like other people bought matches and now he couldn't remember which one it was or where he might have left it. Under his bed? On the lavatory cistern? In the cocktail cabinet?

'Find it,' he ordered, and the bodyguard and the secretary and the housekeeper ran all over the house trying to follow the sound.

It was Mr Sprott who reached it just as it was about to stop ringing. It was under a pile of monogrammed underpants in his chest of drawers.

'Hello!' he shouted. He was a man who always shouted into telephones. There were some strange noises; a sort of gulping sound followed by a gabble. 'Speak up, damn you. I can't hear you!'

'It's me, Daddy. It's Lambert. I've been kidnapped! You've got to come and get me!' More gulping, more tears. What a cry-baby the boy was!

'All right, Lambert. I'll come and get you, but where are you? Speak clearly.'

'I'm on an island. It's an awful place—'

'What island? Where is it?'

'It's in the sea.'

Stanley Sprott rolled his eyes. 'Yes, Lambert, islands are usually in the sea. But where? Which sea?'

'I dunno – they won't tell me – but it's cold. There aren't any coconuts. I've been phoning and phoning you every day.' He broke off, gulping again. 'My battery is running out.'

'Lambert, please think. Are there any other islands near by?'

'There's a couple on one side.'

'What side. East? West? North? South?'

'I dunno. The sun comes up behind them, I think. It's awful here – it's weird. There's these aunts; they're mad and they give me drugged food. You've got to come, you've got to! There's one after me now!'

The line went dead. Mr Sprott stood for a while thinking. An isolated island with two islands to the east of it. And – unbelievably – a posse of aunts.

He gave his orders. 'I want the *Hurricane* made ready. I'll pick her up at London docks. Get a couple of armed men aboard and see there's plenty of ammunition. Pick them carefully; this mission is secret!'

103

The *Hurricane* was his yacht – a converted patrol boat and his pride and joy.

It was only then that he went to the police. He would not trust them to find Lambert – that job he would do by himself without telling anybody – but he might as well find out if there were any other clues.

That evening a third picture appeared on the walls of the police station, and in bus shelters and public libraries. This was of Aunt Myrtle, as remembered by the housekeeper and the man who fed the seals in London Zoo. It was even more peculiar than the other two pictures. Aunt Myrtle seemed to be standing in a high wind with her mouth open, and once again no one came forward to say they had seen her.

But Stanley Sprott's team of researchers were already marking down all the islands in the North Sea and the Atlantic with two islands to the east of them. And the *Hurricane*, with a full complement of arms on board, lay ready at the docks.

Chapter Ten

He seemed to be swimming quite slowly and peacefully, though the swell he left as he moved through the water could be felt on shores a thousand miles away.

Above him, the air was filled with flocks of birds which circled him, and the sea creatures ringed him down below. The sky was a hazy gold and the sunsets were glorious and lingering, as though the sun could not bear to go down on such a sight, and the sea glittered and glistened.

As he swam, the kraken hummed, but not all the time. Sometimes he stopped and turned his head to speak to someone who was swimming close beside him and when he did that, the birds in the air fell silent and the underwater creatures moved their fins and flippers carefully, so as not to make a splash. Because the person who was swimming beside the kraken was important, and they wanted to make sure that he understood what the kraken was telling him.

Strange things happened as the kraken moved south from his Arctic hideout. He came level with an oil rig where men were working the night shift. The lights of the rig were only distant specks to the kraken but he paused and changed his Hum to a deeper one, and on the rig a man called Dave O'Hara said:

'I'm going to shut off the waste pipe.'

His mates put down their beer mugs and stared at him.

'Why? What's got into you? It's always on at night.'

This was true. The outlet pipe spilled its filthy sludge into the water night and day.

'I dunno,' said Dave, 'but I'm shutting it off.'

And he did so . . . and the kraken swam on.

On the Island, Herbert was the first to know.

His mother had come out of the sea a few days before and had tried to nag him again.

'You must make up your mind, Herbert,' she had said in the selkie language they spoke when they were alone. 'You're not young any more; and I won't be around for ever. If you're going to stop being a seal and start being a man you must do it now.'

For a while, Herbert only looked at her. Then: 'Listen!' he said in his quiet and serious voice.

She had listened, and she had heard it because selkies are famous for the sharpness of their ears. Not the Great Hum with which the kraken sent out long-distance messages, but the quiet, thrumming noise he made when he was patrolling the ocean.

'This is not the time to be human, Mother. I shall greet him in the water, and proudly, as a seal.'

It was because of Herbert that Myrtle understood more quickly than the other aunts how near the kraken was. She had tried to play Herbert one of his favourite pieces – a minuet by Mozart. Usually he listened to this with his eyes closed, absolutely enchanted; Mozart was his favourite composer. But now he was restless, eagerly looking out to sea, and then he shook his head once as if to excuse himself and dived into the waves.

Soon it wasn't only Myrtle who guessed. Aunt Etta saw three snow geese – birds she had never seen on the Island before – and Coral came back from a shell hunt, dancing with excitement.

'The sea is changing colour,' she said. 'Only slightly, but it's changing.'

Then suddenly it seemed as though everyone knew that the time was coming and the last-minute preparations began.

In his bed, the old Captain sat with the telescope glued to his eyes and tried to be gloomy.

'Of course he won't be like the kraken was in the olden days. He'll be smaller, like the seals are smaller and the sheep, and the bosoms of the ladies. Maybe he won't be any bigger than a whale,' said Captain Harper. But if anyone tried to take the telescope away from him he became absolutely furious and, as the kraken came closer, he scarcely slept.

As for the aunts and the children, during those days they seemed to be welded together into one band of workers who thought of nothing except to make the best possible welcome for the kraken when he came. It was impossible to imagine that Fabio and Minette had been drugged and kidnapped against their will not three weeks before. There was no need to give them orders; they knew what needed doing almost as soon as the aunts and they, like the aunts, never spared themselves.

Then one day they too heard the Hum once more.

It was the kraken's Daily Hum, his Working Hum, the Hum with which he cleaned and healed the sea, and it was getting closer, and closer . . .

There was only one thing which puzzled the aunts. Every so often the Hum stopped and they heard a low rumbling which might have been the kraken speaking. They couldn't understand the words from that great distance – and in any case none of the aunts spoke Polar – but they could understand the tone, and the feeling they had was that whoever the kraken was talking to was driving him a little mad.

But who could it be? The kraken had always been a loner.

They were soon to find out.

Chapter Eleven

The Great London Aunt Hunt was still going badly. The pictures of Etta and Coral and Myrtle went on flapping on the walls of police stations everywhere but the people who came to say they had seen one or other of them were obviously barmy. A man came and said a lollipop lady who was helping school-children across the road in Kensington had a moustache and was certainly Aunt Etta, but she wasn't. Another man said he had seen Aunt Myrtle busking outside a cinema, but he hadn't. And anyone weighing over a hundred kilos and wearing jewellery was apt to be hauled off by the police in case she was Coral.

'Don't call me "aunt",' terrified women were begging their nephews and nieces all over London's streets and, by the time the children had been gone three weeks, the word had almost disappeared.

Minette's mother, as the days passed with no news, smoked three packets of cigarettes a day, couldn't sleep without slurping a full tumbler of whisky and allowed her flat to get into even more of a mess than before. Of course in some ways it was easier without Minette who kept trying to tidy up and open windows. All the same, Mrs Danby couldn't help wishing she had let her have a nightlight.

'And I should have taken her to the seaside – she always wanted to go,' she said to her latest boyfriend.

'You can take her when she comes back,' he said, dropping his empty lager can over the side of the sofa. 'Though I've never seen much point to the seaside myself. The water comes in, the water goes out – what's the sense in that?'

Professor Danby too wished he had done some things and hadn't done others. He had promised every time she came to take Minette to the ice rink and there'd never been time, and he'd known really that she didn't want an encyclopaedia without pictures for her birthday.

But when they telephoned each other for news of Minette, the Danbys quarrelled as much as ever. They had decided that she had run away, and of course they blamed each other.

'I'm surprised she lasted so long in that pigsty you live in,' the professor said.

'Well, really,' Mrs Danby would reply. 'Considering that your place would make an underground tomb on a rainy Sunday look like Disneyland, you've got a nerve!'

The Mountjoys were not sorry about anything they had done. They were sure that Fabio had had everything he needed in their house and that in sending him to Greymarsh Towers – and *paying* for it – they had treated him better than any poor child from the back of beyond had a right to expect. But they did wonder whether they should tell Fabio's mother that he had disappeared, and his other grandparents in South America.

'I really can't face the thought of having a lot of

110

foreigners coming here and waving their arms,' said Mrs Mountjoy. 'They probably paint their faces and don't wear shoes.'

Old Mr Mountjoy agreed. 'Still, she is the boy's mother. We'll give it a few more days and then if there's no news we'll have to let them know.'

Both the Mountjoys and the Danbys were angry with the police. 'You've gone cold on the case,' Mrs Danby accused the superintendent.

But she was very wrong. Discovering the third kidnap and the third aunt had given the police a new and important lead. Two days after Stanley Sprott came to report that his son was missing, an 'Aunt Myrtle' was seen in Putney swimming baths. She had long greyish hair and an open mouth, which is a silly thing to have in a swimming bath, so it had to be her.

The police wearily pulled her in and sent an officer to Mr Sprott's house to ask the housekeeper to come and identify her – and learnt that Mr Sprott wasn't there.

So where was he, they wanted to know. He was supposed to be standing by in case there was news of Lambert.

At first no one would tell him, but when the policeman threatened to get a search warrant, the secretary admitted that he had gone away in his yacht.

'That'll be the *Hurricane*,' said the superintendent thoughtfully when the officer got back to the station.

They knew a bit about Mr Sprott's activities and his yacht.

'I think we'll see what he's up to. He may have got a lead on the boy.'

'What about the other parents – it's likely the children are all together. Should we tell them?'

'Not yet. If we find them we'll bring the parents out by helicopter. But we won't say anything yet.'

The team that Stanley Sprott had sent to the chart room at the British Museum, to look for lonely islands with two islands to the east of them, had found an ancient map with three that seemed likely.

Now the *Hurricane* was steaming to the first of these – a place called Dooneray off the west coast of Scotland. It was a small island and there were no houses marked on it, but it seemed quite likely that the mad aunts who held his son were keeping him imprisoned in a cave.

As he paced the deck, Stanley Sprott was wondering about the ransom. Why had no one asked him for money in exchange for Lambert? Not that he'd have paid it – he'd have blown the kidnappers to hell before he wasted money like that – but it was odd. Everything was odd about this child snatch.

Though Mr Sprott was wearing a uniform – a navy cut reefer and a cap covered in gold braid – he never did any real work on the boat. He had a captain who sailed it, and two crew members to whom he kept shouting orders which they ignored. If they hadn't, they would have run aground many a time because Mr Sprott had no real knowledge or understanding of boats.

The *Hurricane* had all the silly things on board that one finds on boats that are rich men's toys: a jacuzzi with gold taps, a vast bed covered with a leopard skin and a lounge with a built-in cocktail bar.

But the boat itself wasn't silly. She'd been a patrol boat belonging to Naval Intelligence and she had all the latest electronic aids to help her find her position. She also had something unusual; an outsize hold with reinforced sides in which Mr Sprott carried things he didn't want people to see.

And she was armed. A heavy calibre machine gun was fitted on the stern deck which Mr Sprott said he needed in case of robbers in the Indian Ocean. And though sometimes his passengers were pretty girls who sunbathed and did nothing except giggle and drink cocktails, sometimes his passengers were not silly at all. Like the two men now who were playing cards below deck. Their names were Boris and Casimir and they came from a country where a boy who didn't know how to use a gun by the time he was six years old wasn't too likely to grow up.

And always, whether the *Hurricane* was on a pleasure cruise or on serious business, Stanley Sprott took along his bodyguard, Des.

'There it is,' said the Captain, pointing to a low shape in the sea in front of them. 'That's Dooneray now.'

It was true that the island had no houses, but it had a whole rash of huts – new-looking, wooden ones. And moving round between the huts, and down on the shore, were people. Quite a lot of people.

'They're a funny colour,' said Des, screwing up his eyes.

Des was right. The people were . . . pink. Quite a bright pink which caught the light and glistened a little.

113

The *Hurricane* shut down her engines. There was no pier; they would have to drop the anchor and go ashore in the dinghy.

Some of the pink people looked up and waved.

'I'm not going ashore,' said the first mate. 'I'm not going if it costs me my job. Someone else can take the dinghy.'

'Nor me neither,' said Des. 'I'll do anything for you, boss, but I'm not going to land among that lot.'

'You'll do exactly what I tell you,' said Stanley Sprott. But he didn't speak with quite his usual venom. To tell the truth he too was looking a little sick.

No one could have been nicer than the leader of the pink people. He had a friendly smile and he introduced his wife, who was called Mabel, and his cousin, whose name was James.

But he wouldn't put on any clothes. None of them would put on any clothes.

'I'm afraid you must take us as you find us. This is a nudist colony; we believe most strongly that our Creator wants us to keep our bodies open to the air and light. In fact we would be grateful if you too would take off your clothes. It is a rule of the island that no one who comes here keeps his skin muffled in unhealthy garments.'

Behind him, in the dinghy, Casimir giggled and Mr Sprott turned to glare at him. Then: 'Rubbish!' he said. 'Now listen carefully: I've got you all covered.' He pointed to the two gunmen in the boat. 'And I want every man, woman and child to line up over there. I'm looking for a missing boy and I'm going to

114

search every nook and cranny, so don't try to hide anything or I'll blow you all to hell.'

'We wouldn't dream of it,' said the leader politely. 'But can't we offer you some lunch?'

Mr Sprott shuddered. On a patch of grass a group of people with nothing on were frying sausages over an open-air grill. He had never seen anything so dangerous.

A terrible hour followed. The pink people went on being polite and friendly but they still wouldn't put on any clothes. They let him go where he liked – into their sleeping huts, their communal dining room, their gym . . . Though he knew really that if Lambert had been held by mad aunts who were nudists he would have mentioned it on the telephone, Mr Sprott felt obliged to search every inch of the island, and made Des search with him.

When they left, the leader presented them with a bunch of sea thrift and an oyster.

'Go in peace, friends,' he said.

As they set a course for the second island on their list, Mr Sprott was not in a good temper. Mr Sprott in fact boiled and snorted and raged and swore that he would get the pink people arrested and deported and imprisoned, which was silly of him since the nudists had every right to be where they were. As for the policemen manning the fishing boat which was following the *Hurricane*, they laughed so much that they could hardly keep a straight course. They had watched Mr Sprott's landing through their binoculars and thought it was the funniest thing they had ever seen.

Chapter Twelve

Minette woke early and immediately decided that she had to wash her hair. She didn't usually wash it before breakfast, but on this particular morning she knew it had to be done.

When she'd finished she draped a towel round her head and went in to see Fabio. He was polishing his shoes. Not the sneakers he'd worn ever since he came to the Island, but his smart shoes; the ones he'd been wearing when he was kidnapped.

He said nothing about her hair and she said nothing about his shoes and they went down to breakfast. Minette half expected Aunt Etta to be cross with her – Minette's long hair took ages to dry and when it was at all windy the aunts made her stay indoors till it was done. But Aunt Etta, sitting as usual behind the porridge pot, only said, 'Good morning' – and then both children found themselves staring at her in a way that was undoubtedly rude.

She was wearing her usual navy-blue jersey and her usual long navy-blue skirt and they were sure that underneath it she wore her usual navy-blue knickers.

But pinned to her jersey was a bow. The bow was made of pink velvet with white spots and after this amazing sight they knew that what they had felt when they got up was real.

What happened next was that Myrtle came in, looking windblown and agitated and said, 'Herbert's gone.'

Aunt Etta merely nodded. If it was true that the time had come, Herbert would have gone out to meet him at sea.

Then Coral appeared, wearing almost all her jewellery and a wreath of dried thongweed in her hair.

'There's a naak in the loch,' she said. 'A funny sort of fellow. The stoorworm won't be pleased.'

Naaks are Estonian; they are the ghosts of people who have drowned and are apt to be silent and grim. This one, Coral said, was the ghost of a school-teacher.

'One of those strict ones with a cane, I should imagine,' she said, 'though it's not easy to tell under water.'

The arrival of the naak all the way from Estonia made it certain. If the ghost of a drowned school-teacher with a cane had come nearly a thousand miles to welcome the kraken, he must be coming very soon.

It was the strangest of days. Everyone was violently excited but they didn't dare to say aloud what they believed.

The stoorworm insisted on being wound round a tree by the north shore so that he could get a good view and, just when Fabio had fixed him up, he decided that the kraken would come straight into the bay by the house and asked to be unwound again.

'Wait for me, wait for me,' shouted Old Ursula to the other mermaids, and this time they did wait for the poor old thing and swam out to the rock they had chosen, holding Walter aloft, and sat there practising a song that Myrtle had taught them. It was a Lapp reindeer-herding song and not particularly suitable but it was the most Northern song that Myrtle had been able to find.

In Art's kitchen, the iced buns he'd made from the boobrie's egg overflowed the larder, were stuffed into flour bins . . . and still they came from his oven.

The Sybil's face turned from blue to purple; her washed feet glistened in the light.

The Captain had pushed his bed right against the window and wouldn't take time off even to eat.

Only Lambert felt nothing and noticed nothing and spent the day crouched over his telephone trying to get through to his father, even though his battery was now completely flat.

By the late afternoon the shore was packed with creatures of every sort. Like people lining the route of a royal wedding or a funeral, they had come early to get a good place from which they could see. There were sea otters and jellyfish, there were anemones and starfish peering out of their pools; there were shoals of haddock and flounders and codlings . . . Some of the animals lined the north shore, others waited in the bay by the house; the birds and rabbits and mice and voles watched from the hill. The children could hardly eat their tea and the aunts did not nag them. They too were having trouble with Art's boobrie buns.

The sun began to dip behind the horizon. The Hum, which had been steady all day, began to change its rhythm and every so often there was this strange gap filled with a kind of exasperated rumbling.

'Please don't make us go to bed,' begged Minette, and Fabio said he wasn't *going* to bed and if they tried to make him there'd be trouble.

But when darkness came and the old clock in the kitchen struck nine, and ten, and eleven, everyone lost hope. At midnight the children went to bed of their own accord; the lugworms and the water fleas and the starfish crawled back into the sand or burrowed under stones. On their rock, the mermaids stopped singing and the boobrie fell silent on her nest.

'We must have been mistaken,' said the aunts bleakly – and they too went to bed.

But when they woke in the morning, there was a new island out in the bay.

The island slept. It slept the sleep of the dead after the long journey – and round it and on it and under it, the creatures who had come with it slept too.

The Hum had stopped. Only a slight sighing, a soft soughing, could be heard as he drew in breath and let it out.

For the watchers on the shore, this second welcome was different from the first. It seemed to have nothing to do with velvet bows and polished shoes. It came from somewhere deeper down.

Fabio and Minette stood side by side, half hidden by an old bent alder which grew by the brook where it ran into the sea. They couldn't find any words. There weren't any to find. The aunts, down on the shore, were holding hands like children.

On their rock, the mermaids were not singing and when Walter began to grizzle, Loreen shushed him angrily. For the kraken slept and the excited welcome they had planned had become a vigil. No one would wake the great beast: not the naak with his cane, not the boobrie on her nest; no one.

They waited for one hour, for two ... The sunshine grew stronger. The sea was turning the most amazing colours, as if a rainbow was hidden underneath the waves, and the air as they breathed in tasted like gorgeous fruit.

'It's like the beginning of the world,' whispered Minette.

And then the kraken sneezed!

Everything changed after that. The moles and the mice and the rabbits on the hill were blown backwards and righted themselves again; Aunt Etta's bun flew from its mooring of hairpins; the boobrie let out a startled squeal ... and everybody laughed.

And the kraken lifted his head out of the water and began to swim very slowly, very carefully so as not to swamp the shore, towards the bay.

He was facing the house now, facing the aunts and the children.

Minette, and Fabio beside her, made exactly the same noise: a gasp of wonder and surprise. For in spite of all they had been told about the kraken – about his goodness, about his effect on the sea, about his healing powers – they had not been able to imagine anything very different from a gigantic whale.

But the kraken's eyes were not in the least like the

eyes of a whale. They were huge and round and golden: to gaze into them was like looking into a lamp which did not burn or dazzle but warmed and comforted. His nostrils were small and deep, but his mouth was large and generous, curving across his face like a bow, and tilted upwards at the corners.

As he moved towards them, the mermaids started to sing, croakily at first, then more strongly. Herbert swam beside the kraken's head, solemn and proud.

And now they saw that his body was not black as they had imagined but dappled in soft colours – the chestnut of a chaffinch's breast, the rose of a stippled trout, the blue grey of a moonstone – all were in his skin as it caught the light.

But he had stopped. He was looking at the aunts. He began to speak.

Unfortunately he spoke in Polar. It sounded like the rumbling and clashing of icebergs and no one understood a word.

Aunt Etta hurried into the house and fetched a megaphone. 'I'm sorry, we don't understand,' she shouted.

But the kraken had already gathered that. He tried again. This time he spoke Norwegian because Norway is further south than the Pole, and he tried only one word but still nobody understood.

'Could you try English?' shouted Aunt Etta through the megaphone.

There was a long pause while the kraken thought about this. Then he took a deep breath and said:

'Children?'

His accent was strange but they understood him perfectly and the relief was tremendous.

'What about children?' yelled Aunt Etta through her megaphone.

The kraken repeated the word.

'Children?' he asked. 'Are there . . . here . . . children?'

The aunts talked excitedly among themselves. Did that mean that the kraken wanted children, or that he didn't?

But anyway none of them were able to tell a lie. They moved over to the alder tree, pulled out Fabio and Minette and led them down to the sand. They didn't even think about Lambert who was still shut in his room. Lambert wasn't a child; he was a stunted adult.

There was a pause while the kraken looked at Fabio and Minette. Have we got it wrong? thought the children. Are we going to be eaten after all?

Then the kraken smiled. It was the most amazing smile; his great mouth curved up and up and his eyes glowed with warmth.

And then he sank and the birds that had been resting on him flew upwards like a white cloud.

He was gone for a few minutes – and when he surfaced again there was someone on his back.

The someone was very small compared to the kraken; not much bigger than a mini car or a dolphin – but it was absolutely clear who he was. He had the same round eyes, the same wide mouth, the same rainbow-coloured skin . . .

But he was worried.

'Will I be all right, Father?' said the kraken's son, as he had said again and again on the journey.

'You will be all right,' said the kraken as he had said

a hundred times. And then: 'Look – there are children to play with and care for you.'

They spoke in Polar but what they said was perfectly clear to everyone. In particular what was clear was the look the infant kraken gave to Fabio and Minette as they stood quietly on the shore.

And to the aunts there came a great thunderclap of understanding. When they had kidnapped the children they had done it because they wanted help, but even at the time it felt strange to find themselves behaving like criminals. Now they realized that there had been a Higher Purpose, as there so often is.

For they understood that the kraken was bringing his child to the Island to be cared for while he circled the oceans of the world, and that he wanted him to be with people of his own age, not elderly aunts.

'We are most truly blessed,' said Aunt Etta. She still had her megaphone to her mouth and the word 'blessed' echoed over the whole Island, and was taken up by all the watchers on the shore.

'Blessed,' nodded the stoorworm, and 'Blessed,' said the naak (but in Estonian) and 'Blessed,' cried the mermaids from the rocks.

Only Minette and Fabio were silent. Minette was remembering how she had wanted to serve the great beast when first she heard of him. Fabio, on the other hand, was wondering what infant krakens *ate*.

Chapter Thirteen

The kraken stayed for several days, resting after his long journey from the Arctic. Mostly he lay quietly in the bay keeping an eye on his child, but just having him there made everything flourish.

The children would run down to the shore barefoot every morning.

'It isn't just that the sand is more yellow,' said Minette. 'It's as if it feels more like itself. Like sand is meant to be.'

It was the same with everything while the kraken guarded them. The turf was greener and springier, the wheeling birds were whiter and the patterns they made in the sky were lovelier.

Everybody on the Island felt it – everyone except Lambert who stayed huddled in his room.

'Imagine we hadn't been kidnapped,' said Fabio. 'Imagine we'd never known there was such a thing as a kraken!'

If the kraken had been anyone else – if he'd been one of those saints whose feet people wanted to touch because they were so holy, or a pop star from whose head silly people tried to cut bits of hair – the aunts would have been worried because absolutely everyone wanted to be where he was. Art rowed out in the little dinghy very early one morning, and they could see him talking earnestly to the kraken's head, and when he came back he was different.

'I told him,' he said to the aunts. 'I never told no one else and I didn't tell you neither, but, well . . . when he opened those great eyes of his I saw it didn't matter, so I'll tell you now. All those years it's been on my mind but I was afraid to come clean.'

And then he told them that he hadn't killed a man at all. He'd been in prison for shoplifting but that didn't seem very exciting so he'd told the lie because he thought the aunts would think him more manly.

'But when I was with him, I reckoned you'd forgive me,' he said – and of course they did, and said that telling the truth was far more manly than killing people, which any creep could do if he set his mind to it and had the right tools.

The stoorworm swam out every day and slithered on to the kraken's back and they could hear the clatter and boom as they spoke together in Icelandic. No one knew what the kraken said to him but when he came back the worm was always calmer and never said anything about being too long for his ideas and needing to be made shorter by plastic surgery.

The mermaids too became different. They left the de-oiling shed and swam round the wonderful beast and sang – and though Oona was still croaky her voice came slowly back as she laid her head against the kraken's hide and the memory of the chinless Lord Brasenott became fainter and fainter.

As for the boobrie, she did something extraordinary. She plucked Aunt Coral's cloak from her shoulders and spread it over the eggs with her beak

125

and then she flapped down to the bay and sat on the kraken's back and honked at him.

She honked for a whole hour and it was hard to believe that he understood her, but he did. She was telling him how sad she was without her husband and asking the kraken to look out for him when he swam on again in case he had lost the way.

'He was always a forgetful bird,' she said.

Herbert hardly came out of the water; he was always close to the kraken in the bay. He had a new strength and dignity now that he knew he would spend his life as a seal, because there is nothing more calming than making up one's mind. Myrtle missed playing the cello to him very much, but she understood. As for Herbert's mother, who was very old now and very frail, she completely stopped nagging him, for she realized that if Herbert had decided to become a man with trousers and a zip he would only have been able get up to the kraken in a boat and speak to him through a megaphone and that would hardly be the same.

But it wasn't just the special creatures, those with a touch of magic in them, who wanted to see and talk to the kraken. Everything that moved or crawled or swam wanted to be with him. Processions of sludge worms, schools of pilchards and puffer fish, platoons of lobsters and countless moon snails, all made their way towards him.

'Is he getting enough rest?' Aunt Etta wondered.

But when she asked the kraken he only turned his marvellous eyes towards her and said (at least she thought he said – his English was rather strange) that there was no living thing he did not welcome.

There were two people, though, who did *not* row out to the kraken and tell him their troubles. Minette did not ask him how to make her parents kind to each other, and Fabio did not ask him how to blow up the headmaster of Greymarsh Towers. This was partly because their past lives now seemed quite unreal to the children, but it was mostly because they were busier than they had ever been in their lives.

For the kraken wasn't just resting. He was watching. And what he was watching was his son. Or rather, he was watching how Fabio and Minette *coped* with his son.

It had been difficult for the kraken, deciding what to do with his child. At first he thought he would put off his healing journey round the world till his son was older. But baby krakens grow very slowly – he would have had to wait for more than a hundred years for the child to grow up, and when he realized what a mess the world was in, he knew he couldn't risk it.

Then he thought maybe he could leave his motherless infant in the Arctic among the walruses and polar bears and narwhals he was used to. But this plan had gone down badly with his son who wanted to travel with his father.

'You can't. It's too far,' the kraken had said.

It takes a year and a day to circle the oceans of the world and it was much too far. The baby swam slowly and often needed lifts on his father's back and no one can really give himself to healing the world when they are worried about their child.

The kraken had heard about the Island and the caring aunts as he heard about everything, and at last he had decided to see if it was a good place to leave his son. But he had not been quite happy. Aunts were fine things but these were aunts without children and the baby kraken needed people of his own age. Or rather people who were a bit older but could remember the troubles and the games and the tantrums of being very young.

Which was why the first word he said when he arrived was 'Children?' and why now he watched Fabio and Minette most carefully out of his golden eyes. If they were not suitable as childminders, he meant to give up his journey and go home. Once you have children nothing matters more than their safekeeping. Every parent in the world knows that.

The baby kraken was not at all like his father. He was still soft and blobby as though his body hadn't quite decided what was going to happen to it. Bulges came out of him sometimes, which were almost arms and legs but not the kind of arms you could do very much with, and not the kind of legs that were much use for walking. He would lose these later and become streamlined and suited to the sea, but at the moment he was rather like a large beanbag and one never knew what kind of shape he would decide to be.

And yet one could see that he was the mighty kraken's son. He had the same large wondrous eyes, the same wide mouth which smiled easily, the same interested nostrils which seemed to hoover up the scents of land and sea.

Like his father, he too could make the creatures of

the sea come to him and when he rested in a rockpool, the barnacles and whelks and brittlestars all seemed to glow with happiness and health.

But there was one thing he could not do.

'Can he *hum*?' Fabio asked on the first day.

They were having lunch. Lambert had bolted his food and rushed back to his room where he lay on his bed with the curtains drawn. He still believed that he was being drugged and that the strange creatures he was seeing were not really there, but seeing a whole *island* that wasn't really there was driving him a little crazy.

Aunt Etta shook her head. 'He's too young. A kraken humming is a bit like a boy's voice breaking; it just happens when he's ready. It's a pity, because that's how krakens speak to each other across distances.'

'Is there any way of teaching him to do it sooner?' asked Minette. 'Could his father . . . ?'

But Aunt Etta said, no – it would just happen when the time was right. She didn't add that his father was worried, knowing that there was no way his child could call him once he went away.

But if he couldn't hum, the kraken was beginning to speak. The trouble for Fabio and Minette was *what* he spoke. With his father he spoke Polar but other languages got mixed up with it, and when he started off in English he quickly wandered off into Norwegian or Swedish or even Finnish which the children did not understand at all.

But Fabio himself had needed to learn English not so long ago and he remembered that what he had learnt first was the name of things to eat.

After that it was easy. For the young kraken did not just feed on the plankton in seawater like his father – he was still growing and needed solid food which he ground up with his gums rather like an old man with no teeth.

'This is a sausage,' Fabio would say, holding up one of Art's bangers and the kraken would repeat 'Soss', or 'Spag' when it was spaghetti of which he was very fond, and of course he soon learn to say 'More' or '*No!*' which all young creatures learn to say very early.

By now he was letting the children play with him in the water, throwing a ball or pretending to hide behind a rock. He would even follow them in the dinghy – but always after a short time he went back to his father and stayed very close to his side, for the bond between those two was very, very strong. And though the great kraken was more certain with every day that passed that he had found the right place to leave his son, his heart was heavy at the thought of the parting that must soon come.

Chapter Fourteen

The next island on which Stanley Sprott landed did not have any naked people on it. It did not have any people on it at all. What it had on it was sheep.

They came to it through driving sheets of rain. It was the wettest rain they had ever come across and it looked as though it must stop soon because the sky would have emptied itself, but it didn't. And on the low-lying, sodden island were hundreds – no, thousands – of soaking sheep.

'There's nowhere to land,' said the skipper.

But when they'd circled the island twice they found a narrow inlet and, chugging up it, they saw a shingle bay where the dinghy could be beached.

No one had wanted to land among the pink nudists and no one wanted to land among the wet sheep.

'The boy won't be there,' said Des. 'No one could last on this dump.'

But Mr Sprott had a bee in his bonnet about a honeycomb of underground caves and tunnels full of mad aunts who were holding Lambert.

'They might have brought the sheep to put people off,' he said, 'or they might come up and shoot them for meat' – and he ordered the *Hurricane* to put down her anchor.

Leaving Casimir to guard the boat they rowed to the island and went ashore.

It was not a pleasant place. Sheep are not often cheerful once they are grown up and these sheep were the wettest, gloomiest sheep you could imagine. They stood pressed together, the water running down their noses, giving off a smell of wet wool and lanolin. Some of them had foot rot and though sheep-pats are not as squelchy as cow-pats, they are not agreeable to walk on in the rain.

'We must go round and round the island in smaller and smaller circles; that way we won't miss any openings. It's like looking for a ball in a field,' said Stanley Sprott.

So they trudged round and round, the water dripping down their necks, slipping and sliding on the wet grass and on the wet other things, while the sheep huddled together, too miserable even to lift their heads, and occasionally made a gloomy bleating noise which did not sound much like *Baa* but more like the crying of doomed spirits in hell. If the mad aunts had brought them to put people off they hadn't done so badly.

'There won't be any caves,' said Des. 'The soil's wrong for caves.'

But Stanley Sprott only told him to keep his mouth shut.

Then, almost in the middle of the island, they did find an opening which led underground.

'Down you go,' said Mr Sprott, very excited. 'Make sure they know you're armed. We'll keep you covered.'

So Des went down into the hole and came back almost at once looking very sick.

'Well? What's down there?'

'More sheep,' said Des, rubbing his behind. 'Rams. Two of them and as mad as hatters.' He turned round so that Mr Sprott could see the jagged holes in his trousers. 'Lucky they didn't get through to the flesh. It can give you rabies, being butted by rams.'

While Stanley Sprott had been pursuing his son among nudists and sheep, the police had been following in a fishing boat. Now, though, they ran into bad weather; fog came rolling in from the west and the skipper of the fishing boat found that his radar was jammed. He insisted on turning into the next port to get it fixed, and this meant that the *Hurricane* steamed on without being tailed.

There was only one island left that fitted Lambert's description. It was a long way away but it had to be the right one; it had to!

'Full steam ahead!' barked Mr Sprott to the skipper, who only raised an eyebrow. He'd had the *Hurricane* doing twelve knots ever since they'd seen the last sheep and he wasn't going any faster till the weather cleared.

Meanwhile in London, Minette's parents and Fabio's grandparents had called a meeting to complain about the police and the feeble way they were handling their case. The superintendent had told the Danbys and the Mountjoys that there was a possible lead on the children's whereabouts and having some hope again brought out all their disagreeableness.

The meeting took place in the Mountjoys' cold house with the brass gong in the hall and the portraits of dead Mountjoys on the wall. The Mountjoys didn't like the look of Mrs Danby, who was as usual chain-smoking and wearing a blouse which showed more than they thought was right. They liked Professor Danby a bit better because he was stern and gloomy like themselves. But the main point of the meeting wasn't to make friends, it was to complain.

'If you ask me, the police are too busy finding homes for dirty tramps and mollycoddling the unemployed to do their job properly,' said old Mr Mountjoy.

He had decided not to send for Hubert-Henry's family after all. His wife had been having nightmares about Indians with poisoned arrows ambushing her in her bed, and her heart was not strong.

Professor Danby agreed. 'Even when they find the kidnappers I expect they'll just send them to prison. In the old days they'd have been hanged, and rightly so.'

The Mountjoys nodded their heads. 'It is absolutely shocking the way this case has been dealt with. Outrageous.'

They decided to complain to their Member of Parliament, and Professor Danby said he would insist on a full inquiry.

Mr Mountjoy approved of that. 'And I shall write to the Minister for Law and Order. God knows what the country is coming to when three children can vanish off the face of the earth without anything being done about it!'

Mrs Danby stubbed out her cigarette and lit another one. 'I'm thinking we might sue the police,' she said thoughtfully. 'Get some money out of them. We might as well have something for the anxiety we've been through.'

Professor Danby was about to disagree with her. He always disagreed with his wife – but this time he didn't.

'It's an idea,' he admitted.

'We could give the kids a good time with the money we get,' said Mrs Danby. She'd buy Minette lots of new dresses and if there was any money over she could do with some new clothes herself. There was a lovely pink georgette with a black underskirt she'd seen at Adrienne's Boutique . . . and the sitting room carpet was getting really shabby.

Professor Danby too was thinking of how he could help Minette with some extra money to spend; her bedroom when she stayed with him could do with a proper writing desk so she could do her homework, and if there was any money to spare he needed the new three-hundred-volume *Grammar Scholastica*. He'd had his eyes on it for months but the cost was absurd.

Even the old Mountjoys thought that suing the police was a good idea. Hubert-Henry's fees at Greymarsh Towers were ridiculously high; any help would be welcome.

They were working out how best to do this when the parlourmaid came in with the tea things on a silver tray. She was the only one who had been fond of Fabio and now she asked whether there had been any news of him.

'No, there hasn't,' snapped Mrs Mountjoy and told her to bring some more hot water. What were servants coming to, sticking their noses into family business?

While the Danbys and the Mountjoys met to complain in London, something sad and serious happened in the city of Newcastle upon Tyne. The mother of Boo-Boo and the Little One tripped on a cracked paving stone and broke her hip.

Breaking a hip is a bad business. An ambulance came and rushed her off to hospital where they put a pin into the joint and told her she had to stay in for a week and be careful for a long time after that.

This left her husband, the tax inspector, with a problem. Being a tax inspector is very hard work. You have to go to an office every day and fill in lots and lots of forms and send rude letters to people who are trying not to pay their tax, and do a great many sums. Betty's husband, whose name was Ronald, was a very good tax inspector and he did not feel he could look after Boo-Boo and the Little One as well as doing his job.

But now something amazing happened. He was just wondering what on earth to do with his children when a tall, fierce-looking lady came striding up the path, carrying a suitcase and the kind of saucepan that people use to stir-fry things in. The tax inspector had never used one because his wife Betty did not cook foreign foods, but he knew it was a wok and once he had realized this, he knew who the lady was. It was Betty's sister Dorothy, who had been imprisoned in Hong Kong for hitting a restaurant owner on the head because he was serving pangolin steaks in his restaurant. She must have kept the wok as a memento and as she came closer he saw that he was right because there was a dent in the side which might well have been made by the restaurant owner's head.

'Where's Betty?' said Dorothy, putting down her case. She did not like her sister Betty, who shaved her legs and had three kinds of toilet freshener in her loo, but families are families and on her way home to the Island she had decided to call on her and see how she was.

She soon realized her mistake. Visiting Betty in hospital was one thing, but being asked to look after Boo-Boo and the Little One was quite another.

'I can't stand children, you know that,' said Dorothy. She could have said, 'I can't stand *your* children,' but she didn't because of Betty being 'family'.

Betty began to cry. Her leg was in plaster and hitched up to something and she had a bruise on her face where she had fallen, so when she cried she looked very pathetic indeed.

'Please, Dotty – oh, please. Poor Ronald works so hard, and he can't give up his job.'

Dorothy didn't like being called Dotty and she didn't like Ronald and she really loathed Betty's house where everything was covered in little crocheted hats or frilly embroidered cloths or sprayed with some gooey scent which climbed into your nostrils and stayed there. Betty's chairs had chair covers and the chair covers had more covers to keep the covers clean, as though sitting down was a dangerous act, and the whole thing drove Dorothy round the bend. Also she was homesick for the

Island and for Myrtle and Coral and in particular for Etta who was next to her in age and her closest friend.

But there was Betty looking absolutely miserable – and after all it wasn't her fault that she was an idiot and had two ridiculous children. Life isn't fair and never has been.

'I'll stay for a week,' Dorothy said. 'Till you're over the worst. But that's all.'

But after a few days Dorothy cracked. Boo-Boo (who was a boy) and the Little One (who was a girl) were the daftest children she had ever seen. They cried if their pyjama cases got mixed up, so that Boo-Boo's sleeping suit ended up in the skirts of the fairy doll and the Little One's nightdress was zipped into the stomach of a fluffy poodle. They cried if she handed them the wrong bath towel so that Boo-Boo had to dry himself on Big Ears and Noddy whereas the Little One was rubbed down in roller-skating Yogi Bears. They threw a tantrum if she brought the cereal packet to the table without its frilly cereal packet container, and they complained because she hadn't combed out the tassels on the lampshades.

'Right, this is it,' said Dorothy on the fifth day. 'I'm going home.'

But when she told Betty, who was still in hospital, her sister cried once more.

'What am I going to do?' she sobbed. 'None of my neighbours seem to want to look after my children.'

Dorothy opened her mouth to tell her why and closed it again. After all, Betty was ill and she was her sister and she wouldn't be able to shave her legs for weeks because of the plaster. On the other hand

138

nothing now could stop Dorothy from going back to the Island.

'I suppose I could take the children with me. Just till you're better.'

As soon as she said it, she wished she hadn't, but it was too late. Betty looked at her gratefully. Usually she would have done anything to keep her darlings from that rough place where the animals wandered in and out of the house and nothing was done *nicely*, but now it was her only hope.

'Thank you, Dorothy,' she said. 'Perhaps the sea air will do them good.'

So the following week Dorothy took the train to catch the steamer to catch the second steamer to catch the ferry which would in the end get her to her home. She did not have a chance to let her sisters know whom she was bringing, which was as well. Even if they had been very badly oiled, Boo-Boo and the Little One would not have been welcome on the Island.

Chapter Fifteen

Minette sat on her bed beside the open window, trying to brush her hair. Aunt Etta insisted on a hundred strokes each night, but now she put her brush down and sighed.

'I'm never going to have children. *Never*. It's awful.'

'Oh come on,' said Fabio, wandering in from the bathroom. 'It isn't as bad as that.'

But it had been very bad.

They had woken early and at once known what had happened. Even before they went to the window they had felt the emptiness and the silence.

Downstairs the three aunts sat stiffly at the breakfast table. Coral looked thinner and Myrtle's blouse was on back to front.

'Go to him,' said Aunt Etta as soon as the children had finished. 'You're excused all your other duties.'

Outside it really hit them. Yet the kraken had only been here just over a week. How could the bay seem so empty, so wrong? And how could such a great beast slip away so silently?

It was all very well for Aunt Etta to say, 'Go to him,' but where was he? Not by the shore, not in his favourite rockpool. The mermaids were guarding the entrance to the bay but the children knew he would not have tried to follow his father. He might

140

be small but he knew what it was to keep a promise.

They found him in the end, half hidden under an overhanging rock. He was almost submerged but his head came up out of the water and he was staring at the open sea. When he saw them, he made the most pitiful sound they had ever heard, a heartbroken moan which ended in a whimper. Like a puppy told to 'stay', when his master leaves the room, the baby kraken waited . . . and looked as though he would wait to the end of time for his father to return.

'Come on,' said Fabio leaning down from the rock. 'It's time for breakfast. We'll go and see what Art has got for you.'

But the kraken only looked at him and then two tears welled out of his golden eyes and rolled into the sea.

He wouldn't eat and he wouldn't play.

'No ball,' he said when they fetched the beach ball and 'No hide an' see.' He wouldn't follow them in the boat, though when they moved away he moaned and shivered even more. In the end they got into the water with him and swam round him rubbing his back and telling him again and again that his father would be back, that they loved him, that he was the last of a great and mighty line of krakens and must try to be brave.

Everyone helped. The mermaids came and sang to him but he only closed his eyes and juddered with sighs. The stoorworm swam out and spoke into his ear.

'To go is to come,' said the worm in his solemn voice.

What he meant was that the earth was round so

that the great kraken was on his way back as soon as he set off. But thoughts about the earth being round were too difficult for the kraken's son, whose tears went on flowing and making the seaweed and the little fish look larger and brighter wherever they fell.

'Do you think if Myrtle played the cello to him it would help?' asked Minette, but it didn't. Although Myrtle had just said goodbye to Herbert, who had gone off with the great kraken, she came at once, but you never know where you are with music. It can make you happy but it can also make you very, very sad.

The children did not dare to leave him alone; whenever they moved away he moaned even more pitifully. Art brought their lunch to the shore and they tried to share it with him but he only turned his head away.

'No soss,' he said when they offered him a sausage roll, and 'No cheeps,' when they handed him the chipped potatoes that had been his favourites.

By the end of the day the children were getting frantic.

'What if he just fades away and dies?' said Minette, close to tears.

'He won't,' said Fabio.

But his eyes were even blacker than usual. People *did* turn their faces to the wall and die; he had seen it in Brazil.

When he had been on his way for a few hours, the great kraken began his Healing Hum once more. Everything was as it had been when he was on the way to the Island. The sky was blue, the air was soft;

above him flew his escort of birds, below him the dolphins and seals circled him.

He drew level with a fishing boat a hundred miles away. The crew had pulled in three tons of tuna and were casting their nets once more to add to the pile of bloodied thrashing creatures on the deck when the captain straightened himself and rubbed his forehead.

'Enough,' he said suddenly. 'We've caught enough.'

His crew stared at him. He was the greediest fisherman in that part of the world; he'd been fined again and again for exceeding the quota.

'You heard me,' he said and the nets were pulled in and the boat turned and headed for home.

But though the kraken went on putting the sea to rights, as he had done before, his heart was heavy. There was an awful emptiness on his left side where his son had swum beside him, and at night his back felt strange without the small bump that had slept on it.

'You're to promise to stay and be good,' he had said to his son, and the child had understood, but it was best not to remember the look in his eyes.

After they had travelled for a day and a night, Herbert came to the front of the kraken's head and said goodbye. It was hard for him to leave the kraken and return to the Island but his mother was getting very weak and he felt it was his duty.

It was even lonelier after Herbert left. Other seals swam with the kraken but they were ordinary seals, not selkies; they did not know his thoughts as Herbert had done.

On a great rock, after another day of swimming, the kraken saw something he had been looking out for. A huge black bird with a yellow beak and yellow feet, huddled up and muddled-looking. He paused and looked directly at the unfortunate bird and, as the kraken's eyes pierced his sadness, the boobrie came to himself again. He remembered that he had a wife who had been expecting eggs and that he had gone to look for food and got lost, and forgotten who he was and where he was going.

Now, as clear as daylight, the boobrie saw the Island and the nest by the loch and his partner waiting and waiting. Why, he might be a father by now . . . and he flapped his wings once and twice and a third time and then managed to lift himself off and to fly away.

And the kraken swam on.

By the third day Fabio and Minette were beginning to lose hope. They had tried everything they could think of to cheer up the little kraken. They used up all Art's washing-up liquid to blow bubbles for him, they invented underwater games, they sang to him and told him stories, but nothing helped. The only thing you could say was that when they left him even for a moment he was worse; moaning more pitifully and watering the sea with his tears.

What worried them most was that he wouldn't eat.

It wasn't just 'No soss,' it was 'No spag,' though he had loved spaghetti, and 'No burgs,' even when Art soused the hamburgers with rich tomato sauce. They watched carefully to see if he was feeding himself from the seaweed and plants by the shore, but he wasn't.

'I can just see him getting thinner every minute,' said Minette, who wasn't looking exactly fat herself.

At teatime Aunt Etta came down to the shore and said enough was enough.

'You're to go up to the house and have hot baths and have your tea in the dining room. You look like something the cat's brought in, both of you.'

'No, please. We can't leave him,' said Minette. 'We want to bring a tent down and spend the night on the beach.'

'Better not keep Art waiting,' was all Aunt Etta said.

So the children had their hot baths and went into the dining room. Art had laid out all their favourite things: sardines and cheese straws and chunks of pineapple on sticks.

And the cake tin was on the sideboard. Poor Art always put the cake tin on the sideboard. He put it out for breakfast and for lunch and for tea, hoping and hoping that someone would manage to eat another bun.

For if one can make seventy-two omelettes from one boobrie egg, it is quite amazing how many buns one can make. Art had made the buns look very beautiful: there were buns with pink icing and a cherry on top and buns with white icing and smarties on top and buns with brown icing and chocolate drops on top – but one by one the aunts and the children had stopped eating them. Boobrie buns are very filling and they just couldn't get them down any more.

Now, as Fabio picked up the tin, Minette said 'No! Absolutely not. I couldn't!'

'I know,' said Fabio. 'I couldn't either. But I wonder . . .'

When they got back to the shore the children took no notice at all of the kraken. They sat down very close to the water's edge and opened the cake tin. Fabio held up a white bun and Minette held up a pink bun. They pretended to eat them, making loud chewing noises.

'Buns,' said Fabio, rubbing his stomach.

And: '*Buns*,' said Minette, sighing with pleasure.

The kraken came closer and watched them.

The children went on pretending to eat buns.

The kraken edged closer still.

'No buns for you,' said Fabio. 'You don't like buns.'

An offended look spread over the kraken's face. He was not used to being left out. He was half out of the water now, his head on the sand.

'Buns?' said the kraken, trying out the word.

Fabio shrugged. 'Well, you can try one, I suppose, but you won't like it.' He picked out a white bun with a big cherry on top and held it up. The kraken studied it . . . opened his mouth . . . shut it. For a moment, nothing happened. Then a glow came into his golden eyes.

'Buns,' said the baby kraken. 'Ah, *buns*!' and opened his mouth once more . . .

When he had eaten seven buns Fabio turned to see Minette crouching on the sand. Her hands covered her face but he could see the tears squeezing out between her fingers.

'Well, really,' he said crossly. 'You'd better *not* have children of your own if you're going to be as wet as that.'

Chapter Sixteen

'If you could go back now – if your parents came to fetch you away, what would you do?' asked Fabio the next day.

Minette felt the familiar crunching in her stomach. Only what was the crunching about? Was it about whether her parents loved her and loved each other, or was it about something else . . . ? Was it about going away from the Island?

'How could we leave him?' she said. 'We'd have to stay till his father came back. It's only a year and a day – less now. We'd have to stay that long, wouldn't we?'

Fabio nodded. 'That's what I think. But if they find us . . .'

They had been playing ball with the little kraken in a rockpool, keeping a close watch because Walter was nearby and sometimes the kraken became muddled and thought the merbaby with his round bald head was a beach ball too.

'I'm not ever going back to my grandparents,' Fabio went on. 'The ones in London, I mean. Not ever. If I have to leave the Island I'm going back to South America. I don't know how, but I'm going.'

Minette nodded. He looked very small, sitting on a boulder with his hands round his knees, but she believed him. Both the children had changed since they came to the Island; they were stronger, and sunburnt, their hair thick and glossy with health.

'Isn't everything beautiful?' said Minette, looking out across the bay. 'Of course it was even before he came, but now . . .'

This was true. It was early summer now; the grass was studded with clover and ox-eye daisies; the rowan which sheltered the house was covered in new green leaves – but it was more than that. It was as though the great kraken's blessing stayed with them, and would stay, even though he himself was gone.

Everyone felt it – and even fewer people went away! The naak did not go back to Estonia; the mermaids, though they had lost all traces of oil, stayed where they were – and the Sybil went on washing her feet.

After the kraken left the Captain had sent for his daughters.

'I can die happy now,' he said, 'because I've seen him. So you can measure me up for my coffin.'

But when the aunts had gone away to cry and came back with a tape measure, they found him and the stoorworm taking tea together.

'If my head is upstairs and my tail is downstairs, where is *me*?' the stoorworm was asking, and it was clear that the old man had changed his mind about dying.

But down on the point, Herbert's mother really was coming to the end of her life. She had chosen the Island as her Last Resting Place, which was a compliment because selkies are fussy about where they die.

'I'm ready to go, Herbert,' she said. 'I'm ready to give myself to the waves.'

And Herbert said: 'The time will come, Mother. Don't hurry it.' But he knew it would not be long now and that when the great kraken returned for his son, Herbert would be free to go away with him.

It was during these peaceful days that they were woken by a sound that was new to the Islanders: a proud and joyful squawking that sent the aunts and children running up the hill.

And there they were! Three chicks the size of bull terriers, their feathers still moist from the egg, their yellow beaks already open as they cheeped and wriggled for food.

'More wheelbarrowing,' was all Aunt Etta said, because with the male boobrie still away the mother would never manage to feed her chicks alone, but the aunts were almost as proud as the bird herself. Boobries have not bred where there are humans for hundreds of years.

Even Lambert had suddenly become almost nice and this was the most extraordinary thing of all. He did his work without grumbling, he ate his food – sometimes he even smiled.

'He too has been touched by the spirit of the great kraken,' said Myrtle, but Fabio disagreed.

'If that creep is being nice there'll be a reason,' he said.

And he was absolutely right.

The battery of Lambert's mobile had suddenly given a spurt of life and he had dialled his father's number. The *Hurricane* was now steaming towards the Island and it so happened that Stanley Sprott heard his phone ringing down in the cabin and answered it.

Mr Sprott knew better than to ask his son anything sensible, like 'What latitude and longitude are you on?' or 'Are there any submerged rocks near the entrance to the bay?' – but there was one question he did ask.

'Those women who are holding you prisoner – are they nudists?'

'Eh?' said Lambert, who did not know what nudists were.

'Are they wearing clothes?' Mr Sprott wanted to know.

Lambert thought about this. 'Yes,' he said. 'They're wearing clothes.'

'And sheep? Are there a lot of sheep?'

Lambert said he didn't think so. 'Just a few on the hill.' Then his battery began to play up again and he said frantically: 'But you're coming, aren't you? You're coming to fetch me?'

'Yes, Lambert, I'm coming,' said Mr Sprott.

It was after he talked to his father that Lambert changed. Soon now the *Hurricane* would come and his father would blow everyone to hell: the creepy aunts, the horrible children and the foul monsters who weren't really there. When Lambert smiled now it was because that was what he was thinking about: all the people he hated lying dead in their own blood.

'I feel sick,' said Boo-Boo, leaning over the rail of the steamer.

151

'I feel sick too,' said the Little One. 'I feel sicker than you.'

Aunt Dorothy looked at them with loathing. What she really wanted to do was throw them into the sea and make her own way to the Island. Doing good is all right when you are beating up restaurant owners or thumping people who are trapping rare animals for their skins, but doing good by taking on your sister's horrible children is just stupid.

The steamer was hardly going up and down but now first Boo-Boo and then the Little One were sick and as soon as they'd finished they started worrying about whether they had messed up their clothes.

'Etta is going to kill me when she sees them,' thought Dorothy.

But though she would very much have liked to throw them both overboard she realized it could not be done so she took them down into the cabin and dabbed at the Little One's velvet coat collar and Boo-Boo's silly blazer, and told them to lie down till they landed.

But landing was only the beginning. After that they had to take a ferry to a smaller island and then they had to wait till the one fisherman who could be trusted not to gape or gawp or give away the secrets of the Island could take them across at night. There was no one else the aunts ever used – and just how sick these idiotic children would be in an open boat at night was anybody's guess.

The *Hurricane* came in quietly at noon. She anchored to the south of the Island, hidden from the house by a copse of windblown trees, and Mr Sprott took Des and one of the gunmen with him in the dinghy for a reconnaissance.

But even if she had come into the bay by the house no one would have seen her. Fabio and Minette had taken the kraken to the north shore with a picnic and the aunts were visiting the Sybil, which they did once a week to see that she was eating properly. Even the Captain was not looking through his telescope but dozing quietly in his bed.

Mr Sprott had at first meant to come in with his cannon firing but then he had thought better of it. After all, Lambert had to be got out safely first.

As the dinghy rounded the spur of rocks, with its row of slumbering seals, he saw a boy standing alone on the edge of the sea.

'It's Lambert!' said Des.

And it was!

Whatever plans Mr Sprott might have made were set aside as his son waded towards him and threw himself weeping into his arms.

'Take me away, quick. Take me to the *Hurricane*. Oh hurry, please, Dad.'

Mr Sprott pulled himself out of Lambert's clinging arms and looked at his son. He looked well. In fact he looked better than he had ever seen him look; but that was neither here nor there. The boy was obviously terrified.

'It's an awful place. They feed you poisoned food and then you see things,' sobbed Lambert.

'What sort of things, Lambert?'

'Creepy crawly things . . . things that slither, and freaks with tails – only they're not really there.'

There was a sudden yell from Des. The bodyguard

knew that it was as much as his life was worth to yell when they were trying to get into a place unseen but now he stood up in the dinghy and pointed with staring eyes at a rock sticking out of the water.

'My God,' he shouted. 'Look, guv'nor! It's a bloomin' mermaid!'

'No, it isn't,' cried Lambert. 'She isn't really there. It's because of what you've eaten. None of them are there, the other one isn't there and the old one isn't there and the long white worm isn't there. They're all because of what Art put in the—'

'Be quiet, Lambert,' said his father. Then to Des, 'Catch her.'

Des didn't need to be told twice. He slipped off his holster and dived into the sea.

The girl was Queenie, and she thought the whole thing very funny. She waited till the clumsy man was almost up to her – then she gave her silvery laugh and vanished underneath the waves.

'She isn't there, she isn't there,' Lambert went on yelling. 'It's what you've eaten – it's Art's seaweed flour.'

'Don't be silly, Lambert,' said his father. 'I haven't eaten any seaweed flour and I saw her quite clearly. Unless it was a trick. It must have been a trick, but if so it was a good one.'

Des was still thrashing about in the icy water. Now suddenly he dived down, grabbed at some-thing – and missed. But when he swam back to the boat he had two things clutched in his hand. A silver fish scale and a golden hair.

Mr Sprott examined them. Then he turned to his son.

'Now then, Lambert,' he said. 'Just tell us what else you've seen on the Island.'

'I haven't seen it – it isn't—'

'All right, boy. Tell us what you *haven't* seen, then. Tell us carefully.'

By the time Lambert had finished babbling about old mermaids with no teeth and long white worms that sucked peppermints and outsize birds the size of elephants – all of which *weren't there* – Mr Sprott's face wore a look of eager cunning. Of course it was probably all rubbish, but if it wasn't, the money one could make! And those trees with the branches stripped off – the ones that Lambert called stoorworm trees – they were there all right.

'Go on, what else?' he prompted, digging his son roughly in the ribs.

But Lambert had said all he could. The sight of that island in the bay that hadn't been there at night and then *really* hadn't been there in the morning had frightened him so much that he couldn't say another word, nor about the small island that had broken off from the big one and was around somewhere.

'Please, Daddy, take me home,' he whined. 'Look, there they are; they're coming for me!'

Stanley Sprott looked up. The three dreaded women whose pictures were on the wall of every police station in London were coming towards them.

Aunt Myrtle was in the lead, which was unusual for her. She was carrying a brown paper parcel and she was very nervous – but in a way Lambert was *hers*, just as Fabio was Aunt Coral's, and Minette belonged to Etta, and she felt she had to hand him back herself.

'Good morning,' she said, bracing herself. 'I see you have come to fetch Lambert – he will be pleased to go home. I'm afraid he never quite fitted in.'

Mr Sprott stared at her. The cheek of the woman was unbelievable!

'I've washed and ironed his underclothes and his pyjamas. I wasn't able to take many of his clothes in the cello case but you'll find everything is there.'

Myrtle now felt she had done all she could and stepped back, leaving her sisters to take charge, which they did by asking Mr Sprott if he would care to stay to lunch.

As she spoke, Etta was looking warily over the bay. She had told everyone to stay out of sight as soon as the dinghy had rounded the point but one could never be sure, she thought, not realizing that it was already too late.

'No, don't,' begged Lambert. 'Don't eat anything in there – you'll think you'll see creepy-crawlies.'

'Be quiet, Lambert,' said his father – and told the aunts he would be delighted.

It was a strange lunch. The aunts had been well brought up and though they thought that Mr Sprott was just as nasty as one would expect from someone who was Lambert's father, they were most polite, passing him the salt and pepper and filling up his plate.

'Won't you try a brandy snap?' asked Aunt Coral. 'They were freshly made this morning.'

Mr Sprott took one and decided it was time to come to the point.

'Now, ladies,' he said, smiling his oily smile. 'I have a suggestion to make to you.' He leant forward, folding his hands on the tablecloth. 'I am getting on in years and I need somewhere to end my days – so I want you to sell me this island.'

There was a gasp from Myrtle, and Aunt Etta stared at him in amazement.

'Sell the Island?' said Coral.

'Sell the Island?' said Myrtle.

'*Sell* it!' thundered Aunt Etta.

'I take it it belongs to you, does it not? And Captain Harper?'

The sisters looked at each other. They had never thought of *owning* the Island. It was just there and they looked after it. But now they remembered that their father had in fact bought it from an old couple who could no longer do the work.

'I suppose it does,' said Etta now. 'But there's absolutely no question of selling it.'

'No question at all,' said Coral.

'Oh no, we couldn't do that,' said Myrtle bravely.

Mr Sprott leant back in his chair and smiled. They did not seem to realize that they were completely in his power.

'I'm prepared to offer ten thousand pounds,' he said. 'And that's generous for a miserable little island . . . I mean for a simple unspoilt island with only one house on it.'

He'd get the money back in a month, charging two hundred pounds for helicopter rides to the Island of Freaks. The pretty mermaid was worth a fortune on her own; he'd put her in an aquarium and people would have to pay extra to hear her sing and comb her hair. As for that creepy worm, he could just see the visitors clutching each other and screaming.

He'd have to keep him in a cage with electric wire. It would be a cross between a zoo, a funfair and Disneyland.

'Very well, ladies. Twelve thousand pounds and that's my last word absolutely!'

But Etta had had enough of this unpleasant game. 'I'm afraid we wouldn't sell the island for a hundred million pounds,' she said. 'We regard it as a Sacred Trust. Now if you would care to take Lambert back with you, I will tell Art that he can clear the table.'

'Oh no you won't!'

Mr Sprott's voice had changed. He had become the dangerous bully that he was before. 'I think you have forgotten something, dear ladies. You have kidnapped three children. Abducted them by force. My son and two others. The penalty for kidnapping is life imprisonment – and it might even be hanging. They're thinking of bringing back the death penalty, I've heard. So I really think you'd better sell me the Island – or would you rather I turned you over to the police?'

There was a sudden scuffle at the door.

'You can't! You can't turn them over to the police because they didn't kidnap us.' Minette had run all the way from the North Shore. Her hair was tousled, her clothes were in a mess but what was strange was that she wasn't at all frightened. 'I *asked* if I could come. I asked Aunt Etta if there was a third place and she brought me here.'

Fabio, who had followed her into the room, caught on at once. 'And I wasn't kidnapped either! Aunt Coral saved me from a vile school where they tie you to pillars and try to set fire to your clothes. If

158

anybody says I was kidnapped, I'll thump them!'

'And Lambert wasn't really kidnapped either.' Minette, who never lied, seemed to have gone crazy. 'He tried to steal Aunt Myrtle's chloroform and the fumes knocked him out and Aunt Myrtle brought him along because there was no one at home to look after him.'

Both children stood and glared at him like angry tigers.

What they were saying was rubbish, Mr Sprott knew that. The police would get the truth out of them in no time – but he had changed his mind. It had seemed worth a try to do everything the easy way – buy the island and then do what he wanted with it when they'd all gone. But there were other ways of getting what he wanted.

'Very well, it looks as though I was mistaken. Come along, Lambert, I'll take you home.'

He took the brown paper parcel with Lambert's pyjamas, shook hands politely, and left with his son.

Oh yes, there were other ways of getting his hands on those weird beasts, thought Stanley Sprott. Before he'd finished they would wish they *had* sold him the island, because what was going to happen now would not be pleasant at all!

Chapter Seventeen

Meanwhile, in London, Minette's parents had found a better way of making money than suing the police.

Mrs Danby thought of it first and Professor Danby didn't hear about it till he saw a newspaper which the tea lady had brought into the University Common Room.

On the front page was a picture of Minette as a baby in her mother's arms. *Heartbreak Mother Mourns Lost Daughter* said the headline, and underneath the picture were some terribly sad things that Minette's mother had said, like there was no second of the day when she did not feel the pain of being without her daughter like a wound in her side. *She was a little angel* Mrs Danby had told the reporter, and she went on to say that a candle burnt night and day by Minette's bed and would go on burning till she was safely returned.

As soon as he saw the newspaper, Professor Danby rang his wife.

'How much did they pay you for that?' he wanted to know.

'Twenty thousand,' said Minette's mother, 'and no more than I deserve with what I've been through.'

'I don't know how you can bring yourself to talk to a filthy rag like the *Daily Screech*,' said the Professor and slammed down the phone.

But all day he was furious. Twenty thousand pounds! It wasn't as though he wasn't suffering just as much over his lost daughter. He didn't light candles by her bed because of the fire risk but the housekeeper, who was fond of Minette, had bought a bunch of flowers and put them in her room. Of course the *Daily Screech* was out of the question – he wouldn't be seen dead with his photograph in a rag like that – but if the *Morning Gazette* was interested he might say a few words about his sorrow and his loss. There was a photograph somewhere that the housekeeper had taken outside the university in which he was standing beside his daughter wearing his gown and hood. It had come out rather well and made it clear the kind of background that she came from.

Fabio's grandparents were too snobby to talk to any kind of newspaper, but they appeared on a late night television panel to bleat about the lack of discipline in modern life and the feebleness of the police who still hadn't returned their grandson.

And even as Minette's parents were getting rich and Fabio's grandparents were complaining, a helicopter was getting ready to take off from the Metropolitan Police pad outside London. It was a small machine manned only by one policeman and a policewoman – and their orders were clear.

'Remember, if you get a chance to land, it's the two children we want. The aunts can wait. And don't pick a fight with Sprott. We're after the boy and the girl right now, and nothing else.'

As soon as they opened the door of the mermaid

shed, Fabio and Minette realized that something serious had happened.

Loreen lay on the tiled floor, chewing mouthfuls of gum and weeping. In her sink in the corner, Oona looked stricken and pale. Old Ursula was shaking her head and muttering.

'It's my fault,' Loreen wailed. 'I've been a rotten mother and I deserve all I get.'

'What is it?' the children asked. 'What's happened?'

Loreen hiccuped and tried to speak but what with her gum and her sorrow no one could make out what she was saying and it was Old Ursula who said: 'Queenie's eloped. She's swum off with that muscleman who came yesterday and tried to catch her.'

'What muscleman?'

'He came in the dinghy with Lambert's father and Queenie went up to sing to him. We didn't think she fancied him but she's gone.'

A low croak came from Oona as she tried to speak. 'She . . . *didn't* . . . fancy him. She . . . said his biceps were silly.'

But the other mermaids took no notice of Oona, who was trying to make out that Queenie hadn't gone of her own free will. Twins always stuck together and what had happened with Lord Brasenott made Oona think that all men were evil, which was silly.

'I spoiled her,' wailed Loreen. 'She always had the best shells and the prettiest pearls for her hair.'

'Now don't carry on so,' said Ursula. 'It isn't your fault Queenie turned out so flighty.'

'She didn't—' began Oona – but Loreen only put

another piece of gum in her mouth and went on wailing. 'I've been a rotten mother, and it's all my fault,' she said again, and she picked Walter out of the washing-up bowl and slapped his tail though he hadn't done anything except grizzle and whine in his usual way.

'We must tell the aunts,' said Fabio.

'Oh dear, must we?' cried Loreen.

But Old Ursula said yes, it was best to own up. 'Get some wheelbarrows and we'll go up to the house,' she said.

So the children came back with three barrows and Art, because flopping about overland made the mermaids' tails sore, and no one took any notice of Oona who went on croaking that her sister had not *liked* the muscleman.

The aunts were very much upset. Not because Queenie was flighty, which they'd known all along, but because it meant that Mr Sprott now knew that there were mermaids on the Island – and maybe other things too.

'I wonder if he knew before he came to lunch,' said Coral. 'Do you think that was why he wanted to buy the Island?'

'Perhaps he'll come back with photographers?' faltered Myrtle.

Fabio and Minette looked at each other. They had lived in the world outside long enough to know that Mr Sprott might come back with something much more serious than that.

A day passed, and half a night, and then they heard the sound they had been dreading: the noise of a boat coming into the bay. So Sprott was back already!

In an instant the aunts were out of bed. Etta ran for the Captain's blunderbuss, Coral fetched Art's catapult, Myrtle grabbed the long-handled brush she used to scrub her back.

Outside, the night was black and moonless but they could make out the boat nosing in beside the jetty. The engine died . . . the cargo was unloaded . . . and almost instantly the boat went into reverse and moved away.

The aunts, clutching their weapons, peered into the darkness. Then suddenly Etta broke the silence with a great shout and ran towards the jetty. And there, standing tall among her suitcases, was a woman in a long raincoat holding what seemed to be a frying pan.

'Dorothy! Oh my dear, how wonderful to see you!' She hugged her sister, unable to keep back her tears of happiness and relief.

It was only then, as the other aunts came forward, that Etta could make out two small figures standing behind the luggage.

'Good heavens, Dorothy, what have you got there?' she asked, shining her torch.

'You may well ask,' said Dorothy, and pushed Boo-Boo and the Little One forward into the light.

Having Betty's children to stay would have been bad at any time. Now with Queenie gone and everyone so jittery, it was a nightmare.

They were awful children. Not awful like Lambert but awful all the same. It wasn't their fault; they'd

164

been brought up to behave like idiots. Boo-Boo (who was a boy called Alfred) wore a bow tie and kept asking Art for shoe polish.

'It's got to be *tan*, not brown,' he said to poor Art, who was trying to prepare mash for the boobrie chicks and take the Captain his meals and cope with the extra people to feed.

The Little One (who was a girl called Griselda) began to cry straight away because Dorothy had forgotten to pack the hankie with a picture of a flower fairy on it which she kept under her pillow, and both the children were terrified of germs. Fortunately they were so wrapped up in their silly fusses about which pyjama case was which that they didn't even notice the strange animals or the danger they might be in. They just went on dusting the chairs before they sat down in them and looking at themselves in mirrors and complaining because their underclothes hadn't been ironed, exactly as if they were still in Newcastle upon Tyne. If Fabio hadn't been so busy with the kraken his temper would certainly have got the better of him but as it was he hardly saw them.

But having Dorothy made up for everything.

Dorothy knew that there was evil in the world. She had met people like Stanley Sprott and she had seen some dreadful things abroad – 'monsters' that were supposed to be mermaids kept pickled in jars, or deformed beasts put in cages for people to gawp at – but she was not afraid. It was Dorothy who filled the Captain's blunderbuss with carpet tacks and set up tripwires behind the house and showed them how to make a cosh.

But when at the end of the first day Etta took her sister down to see the kraken, the tough, hard-faced woman changed into someone very different.

'Oh Etta,' she breathed, looking down at the little creature as he slept, 'that I should live to see this day!'

Queenie sat in Mr Sprott's bathroom on the *Hurricane* up to her waist in scented water. The bath was a jacuzzi, with water bubbling up from all sorts of places. The taps were gold and so were the shower fittings and on shelves all round were cut-glass bottles full of wonderful things: coloured crystals and glittering hair sprays and creams for making the body firm and more creams for making it soft once it was firm and more creams still for making it not just soft and firm but also pink.

The creams belonged to Mrs Sprott, but she wasn't there so Queenie had the bathroom to herself. It was exactly the kind of bathroom she had dreamt of when she heard stories about mermaids marrying princes and going to live in palaces, but as she splashed more water over her tail, the tears kept welling out of her eyes and she was shaken by terrible sobs. She had never in all her life been so unhappy and afraid.

For Oona had been right. Queenie had not swum away to be with the muscleman. Queenie had been most cruelly caught by Mr Sprott's henchmen and this bathroom was as much her prison as any cell in a cold and dirty dungeon.

She had gone out for a moonlight swim and when she got to the end of the bay she found a net under

166

the water stretched between two rocks. At first she thought the net had been put there by fishermen but as she tried to free herself it was pulled tighter and tighter still, and she was towed away behind the dinghy and hauled aboard the *Hurricane* like a slab of dead meat.

'Oh, why didn't I listen?' cried poor Queenie. 'My mother told me to stay out of the way of men.'

She would have given anything now to see Loreen chewing her gum or Old Ursula with her toothless smile; she even missed Walter. But the person she longed for most was Oona. She understood now how Oona had felt on board Lord Brasenott's yacht; no wonder the poor girl had lost her voice. The round window of the bathroom had a curtain but Des and the two horrible men who guarded the boat had pulled it aside and every so often their faces leered in at her.

'Oh, what is to become of me!' cried poor Queenie, and felt so sad that she wanted to die.

And while Queenie wept in the bath, Lambert snivelled in his father's cabin.

'I don't want a mermaid for a stepmother,' he whined. 'I don't want a mermaid for a stepmother *anyway* and I certainly don't want a mermaid for a stepmother who isn't really there.'

'Don't be silly, Lambert,' said Mr Sprott. 'One doesn't marry mermaids, and anyway your mother is still alive.'

But he sighed deeply as he said it for Queenie was much prettier than Mrs Sprott with her purple hair and her claw-like fingernails and her greedy eyes. Mrs Sprott was a kind of dung beetle, only instead of collecting balls of nice soft manure she collected clothes and shoes and jewels and furs and dumped them in his house before going out for more.

'They'll laugh at me at school if I have a mermaid for a stepmother and I don't like fish. Even half a fish I don't like . . . even a fish that isn't really there,' moaned Lambert.

'Oh be quiet, Lambert,' said Mr Sprott. 'No one's going to marry her. We're going to show her off in a tank and make a fortune out of her. But first she'll have to tell us where the other creepy-crawlies are to be found. I'm going to catch the lot of them and then—'

But he didn't finish what he was going to say. Lambert couldn't be trusted not to blab. Not till the weird beasts were on board and tied up and on their way across the Atlantic would he say anything. He had decided to set up his funfair on an island off the coast of Florida which belonged to a friend. Or rather to a business partner. A man like Stanley Sprott did not have friends.

But first he had to cross-examine Queenie and see how much of his son's babble was true. He found Des ogling the mermaid through the bathroom window, while Casimir and Boris grumbled that it was their turn.

'I found her,' Des was saying. 'So I get the longest turn. She's mine really and the old man ought to—'

He turned to see Mr Sprott standing behind him. 'If any of you lay a finger on this mermaid you'll go straight overboard,' he said, and told Des to board up the window. Then he opened the door and drew up a stool beside the bath.

'Now, dear,' he said, 'I've got a few questions to ask you. It's about your family. You're not alone, are you? You've got a mummy and a daddy?'

'I haven't got a daddy,' said Queenie, pulling Aunt Myrtle's bodice tighter round her top.

'But a mummy . . . and little brothers and sisters?'

'Only one of each and my great-grandmother.'

Queenie was too frightened to realize that she was being trapped.

'And of course there are the other . . . unusual creatures on the Island. Lambert told me about a worm. White, isn't he?'

Queenie nodded. 'He's very clever,' she said.

'And what else is there on the Island?'

Now at last the mermaid saw where this was leading. 'Nothing,' she faltered. 'Just the aunts.'

'Oh, I think there are,' said Mr Sprott. 'Perhaps if I take the plug out of the bath it will help you to think.'

'No! Oh please, no!'

To take water from a mermaid is the most terrible thing you can do. But Mr Sprott had already pulled it out; the water was draining away. Now he picked up the electric hairdryer.

'No!' she cried again, trying to protect her tail from the terrifying heat.

Mr Sprott turned it off.

'You've remembered something else?'

'There's a big bird . . . a boobrie.' Surely he wouldn't want the boobrie? What use would she be to him?

'And where is it to be found? Is there a nest?'

'No . . . I don't know . . . It's up on the hill. Oh please put the water back.'

169

But Mr Sprott did not put the water back – and now he put on the dryer again and let the ghastly heat play over her tail till the freshness of the silver became dull and dead . . . Queenie's tail had been her pride and joy and now it looked as though it had been on a fishmonger's slab for a week.

She held out as long as she could. Then she said pitifully: 'There are some selkies. They're just seals really. There's nothing to them.'

But Mr Sprott wasn't to be fobbed off so easily.

'What sort of seals?' He had dropped the hairdryer. Instead he had taken a pair of scissors and was holding a hank of her golden hair, ready to chop it off. 'Go on – answer. Don't keep me waiting. I don't like to be kept waiting.'

'I don't know,' whispered poor Queenie. 'It's just stories. People say they can turn into humans if someone drops seven tears into the water or if they're touched with cold steel.'

Mr Sprott's eyes glittered. He saw the circus ring . . . a seal on a tub . . . then a sharp pronged fork in its backside and lo, a woman jumps down. A transformation scene, better than a pantomime.

'Go on – what else is there? What else?'

But though he threatened her again with the hairdryer Queenie kept silent about the little kraken. For she knew that the end of the kraken meant the end of the sea as she knew it – and thus the end of her world – and Mr Sprott did not dare to hurt her any more or she wouldn't be worth putting on show.

'I'll speak to you again tomorrow,' he said, turning the water on again. 'Don't think I've finished with you, because I haven't.'

170

But as he gave his orders – the hold to be cleared, reinforced nets and lifting gear to be got ready, and harpoon guns to stun the beasts before they were hauled aboard – he did not realize that the greatest prize on the Island was still unknown to him. Neither Queenie nor Lambert had mentioned the kraken's son.

Chapter Eighteen

The great kraken had reached the warmer southern seas. The fishes who joined him were brilliantly coloured, with fan tails and exotic spikes, and from the islands flashing birds with crests of crimson and orange came to welcome him and perch on his back. The water was clear and calm and the corals on the sea bed were of every colour under the sun.

As he swam the great kraken hummed his Healing Hum, and the turtles who had lumbered out of the sea to lay their eggs on the sandbanks were left in peace, and the rich men who had come to slaughter the porpoises pulled in their harpoons as the swell made by the kraken's passing reached their boats.

Yet the kraken was not happy. The dolphins and seals that swam round him felt this and were puzzled. He was smiling less; his golden eyes sometimes had a clouded look.

But why? He did not know – only that somehow he felt uneasy. He was missing his son of course, but there could have been no safer place to leave him than the Island of Aunts.

'I must pull myself together,' thought the kraken. 'I do not belong to myself; I belong to the sea.'

And he put aside his vague and troubled thoughts and swam on.

*

Two days after Boo-Boo and the Little One came to the Island, Old Ursula disappeared. She had swum out to say goodbye to Herbert's mother and never came back.

The other mermaids were frantic.

'I should have been nicer to her,' wailed Loreen. 'I shouldn't have said her tail smelt. It did smell but I shouldn't have said it.' And Oona wept because time and again she'd left the old creature flapping in the sink instead of helping her.

As for the aunts, they now knew once and for all how great was the danger they were in. Great-grandmothers do fall in love but they aren't often silly about it when they do. Old Ursula could not have eloped, she must have been snatched – and that meant that Queenie too had been taken by force. And sure enough, when they searched the bay, they found a net stretched between two rocks.

'We must have a Council of War,' said Etta, and made everybody do thirty press-ups so as to make the blood go to their heads and help them to think.

But even with all the blood in their heads, they knew that fighting off Sprott and his men would be almost impossible and that their only hope would be to get the animals to hide.

'The storworm must stay at the bottom of the loch – no coming up for chats,' said Coral.

'And Herbert and his mother should come closer to the house,' said Myrtle. 'They could have the pond in the vegetable garden.'

Art offered to guard the mermaid shed with the Captain's blunderbuss – secretly he still hoped he might have a chance to kill someone after all – and they decided that the Sybil must be brought indoors; she was far too loopy to be left on her own.

But it was easier to decide what should be done about the creatures than to get them to do it. The stoorworm pointed out that he was after all a wingless *dragon* and should be helping to guard the Island, not skulking about in the bottom of lakes, and Herbert wouldn't bring his mother any closer because she wanted to die beside the sea and not in somebody's Brussels sprouts.

But of course it was the kraken that they worried about most of all, and it was now that the aunts wished from the bottom of their hearts that they had never kidnapped Fabio and Minette.

They knew exactly where the little beast could be hidden. In a large underwater cave, a kind of grotto on the North Shore with only the smallest opening on to the strand. It was a beautiful place, with a pool of clear, deep water surrounded by gently shelving rock, and at the back of the grotto was an opening to the cliff which gave enough light to see by. The opening came out by Ethelgonda's burial ground and the naak had promised to keep watch up there.

But to keep the kraken in a cave when he was used to the freedom of the sea would not be easy. He would need people all the time. And people, to the kraken, were Fabio and Minette.

'There is no question of you staying alone with him through the night,' said Etta firmly. 'My sisters and I will take shifts.'

'Yes there is. We'll take a blanket and lots of food – but we're going to do it. It's our job,' said Minette.

'It's not your job to risk that kind of danger.'

But something odd was happening to Fabio and Minette. Perhaps it was from living on the Island among creatures that did not need to speak very much, but they seemed to know each other's thoughts.

'If you didn't want us to do our work you shouldn't have kidnapped us,' said Minette.

And Fabio, between gritted teeth, said, 'Nothing is going to stop us being with the kraken. Nothing.'

By nightfall, everyone was at their posts: Art guarding the mermaids, Coral crouched by the boobrie's nest, which they had ringed with barbed wire; the Sybil zooming round the house muttering about wind-chill factors and burning the Captain's semolina.

And the kraken hidden in his secret place beneath the cliff.

The children had lit candles and put them on the ledges, and the flames flickering on the stone lit up the colours of the rock.

'It's like Merlin's crystal cave,' said Minette dreamily, and she was right. Because the kraken was his father's son, all sorts of creatures came to be near him in the water: crimson crabs and clusters of pipefish and families of sea mice . . . But if it was beautiful in the cave, keeping the kraken quiet and happy was hard work. Fortunately he was learning English so fast that they could sing to him and tell him stories.

'More *Snow White*,' he would command, or 'More *Puss in Boots*.'

But the stories he liked best were the ones they

made up about his father – about the great kraken and his adventures as he swam though the oceans of the world.

Where the sides of the grotto sloped to the water there was one place which was almost flat and it was there that the children had made a kind of camp. They had brought sleeping bags and plenty of food and of course the tin of boobrie buns. If the kraken got restless and swam too near the opening of the cave, they only had to bang with a wooden spoon on the tin and he would hurry back, his mouth already open for his treat.

Even so, the aunts were worried about them and, sometime in the small hours, Etta and Dorothy stopped patrolling the Island and went down to the grotto again, determined to make the children come up to the house and go to bed.

The kraken was asleep, his head just out of the water. And on either side of him, curled up on the ledge so that their arms were almost touching him, slept Fabio and Minette.

And the aunts turned back and said nothing, for it was clear that these three lived in a circle of friendship that nothing now could break.

There was no attack from Sprott's people that night, but just before dawn something did happen.

Down on the point, Herbert's mother slipped quietly from life. Her eyes filmed over; she sighed deeply, her whiskers trembled . . . Then she spoke her son's name once – not in the selkie language but in proper human speech so that Myrtle too could understand.

176

'*Herbert*,' said Herbert's mother. She didn't say anything more but from the way she said it they knew that she thought Herbert had been a good son and she was thanking him. Then she hoisted herself slowly to the very edge of the rock, lifted her head once towards the sky – and gave herself to the sea.

It was a beautiful death – exactly the kind of death the old seal had chosen – but of course for Herbert it was a moment of great sadness, and when it was over, Myrtle would not leave him even to get her meals.

Her sisters were worried about this. Myrtle had always felt things too much. When she was small she had tried to bring a tin of sardines back to life by floating the headless fishes in a wash basin, and they did not think she should be out on the point on a night when there might be danger.

But Myrtle in her own way was obstinate.

'I can't leave Herbert alone with his sorrow,' she said – and she wrapped her legs in an old grey blanket and settled down beside her friend.

There was a time when Queenie would have hated sharing a bath with old Ursula but now she was touchingly glad of her company. The old mermaid was as tough as old boots and she didn't give a fig for Mr Sprott's threats.

'He can't do anything to me. I'm old and I don't care,' she said.

Mr Sprott hated her. She spat at him and cursed him and tried to bite him with her single tooth, and when Des came anywhere near she screeched at him.

'Don't you dare ogle my great-granddaughter you plug-ugly,' she yelled.

'You can't put that old horror on show,' said Des. 'Nobody'll pay to see the likes of her!'

Mr Sprott shrugged. 'Maybe I'll sell her to medical science to be cut up,' he said. 'No one knows how a mermaid's tail is joined to her body.'

Seeing Ursula so angry and unafraid did Queenie good. But of course they both knew what danger they were in. And sure enough, later that evening Boris and Casimir came in with blindfolds which they tied roughly round the mermaids' eyes. Then they were wrapped in coarse sacking and felt themselves raised up, swaying on steel hooks, and then lowered, still swaying horribly, into some deep cold place.

When they could see again, they found that they were sitting in a crude, rusty tank filled with water. The tank was in the corner of a large, dark, empty space, stuffy and evil-smelling. There were no windows and no lamps, and all they could hear was the slap of the water against the ship's sides.

They were in the hold of the *Hurricane* which Sprott had prepared, like a slave ship of old, for his prisoners.

'Don't worry, you won't be by yourselves much longer,' jeered Des. 'Lots of your little friends will be along soon.'

Then he climbed up the steel ladder, pulled it up after him, and shut the trapdoor, leaving them alone in the foul-smelling darkness.

There were five men in the launch: Stanley Sprott himself, Boris and Casimir, and the bodyguard, Des.

178

Lambert had been left behind with the skipper – the poor boy was definitely going crazy – but Sprott had forced the mate of the *Hurricane* to come too.

The launch was towing two large inflatable rafts loaded with equipment, with which to net the creatures and stun them before they were floated out to the *Hurricane*.

All the men had guns and knives and whistles to blow if they wanted extra help and their orders were clear.

'Now remember, if you have to shoot, shoot the aunts, not the creatures. You can't get money for aunts. But don't shoot at all if you can help it. We want silence and we want speed.'

The launch slid on to the sand. The men got out.

Boris and Casimir set off up the hill; they were going for the boobrie and the stoorworm. Sprott himself and the mate made their way to the mermaid shed: Sprott liked the idea of carrying the wriggling, struggling mermaids over his shoulder.

And Des was to capture the selkies.

Des had grumbled about this. 'What do you want a couple of old seals for?' he asked Mr Sprott.

Sprott had not told anyone what Queenie had said about selkies; it was probably rubbish anyway. 'They're supposed to be able to sing,' was all he said.

So Des was not in a good mood as he climbed up the rocks towards the sleeping seals. Even if they could sing it didn't seem very exciting – lots of animals made noises in their throats – and how the devil was he supposed to pick out the selkies from the others?

'There's two of them, lying apart from the rest,'

Lambert had said. 'They've got funny eyes.' And then he'd started to snivel and go on again about how they weren't really there.

But as he got closer, Des saw that Lambert was right. There *were* two seals lying apart from the rest. A big bull seal and a smaller one; a cow probably. He'd tackle the smaller one first and if things went wrong he could always skin the brutes. Sealskins fetched a good price.

Des crept closer. The big seal opened his eyes, and even in the dim moonlight, Des could see that his eyes were not quite like those of an ordinary seal.

But it was the smaller one he was after. She'd been asleep but now she stirred . . .

Really it was uncanny how human she looked. Her body was just a grey splodge and he couldn't see her flippers, but as she yawned and opened her eyes you could almost forget she was a seal.

Des shook himself. He was getting fanciful. Better get her netted and dragged away. It shouldn't be a problem; she was only half grown – he probably wouldn't even need the stunner.

He crept the last few metres, got to his feet – and threw the net.

And the selkie screamed. He had never heard such a scream coming from the throat of an animal. It was a completely human scream and it was all Des could do not to drop the net and run back to the ship.

But he didn't. He cursed and tried to tighten the net while the seal struggled and kicked – and then suddenly the screams had words to them! Proper human words.

'Leave me alone,' shrieked the selkie in her high-pitched voice. 'Let me go at once, you brute. Help! Oh, help!'

Up by the boobrie's nest, Coral got to her feet, vaulted over the barbed wire – all sixteen stone of her – and began to run towards the point. Etta, who had been helping Art to guard the mermaid shed, seized the blunderbuss and did the same. Going to rescue Myrtle was something they did as naturally as they breathed.

But someone else was coming to Myrtle's rescue.

As Des straightened himself to pull the net tighter, something came at him: an enormous wet wall of grey muscle . . . a tank of solid blubber which sent him sprawling. He tried to get to his feet but the bull seal threw back his head and roared and then he opened his mouth and Des saw the evil-looking teeth and felt his hot breath. The creature was going for his throat . . . in a moment it would be all up with him.

Choking, struggling, Des tried to reach his knife but every time it was in his grasp, the seal charged again. Helpless, sprawled on the ground, he tried to cover his face, but the awful teeth were closing on his flesh . . .

Then when he thought his last moment had come, he found the knife, and lunged. The seal reared back and he almost missed . . . almost but not quite. He'd made a nick in the animal's shoulder, nothing more . . . but, my God, what was happening now? It wasn't teeth that were fastening round his throat, it was hands, it was fingers . . .

With a blood-curdling shriek, Des managed to struggle to his feet – and then he ran . . . ran and ran, almost mad with horror . . . ran, with the spittle running out of his mouth, away and away across the Island, trying to escape from what he'd seen. Ran until he stumbled over a gorse bush, and found himself falling . . . falling down towards a pool of dark water far below.

Chapter Nineteen

The stoorworm had always been worried about his thoughts getting stuck halfway down his body.

Now he didn't worry any more. The terrible sadness he felt as he lay curled up in the hold of the *Hurricane* had not got stuck anywhere. It went right down through every single segment to the tip of his tail. He was just a long tube of wretchedness and despair and shame.

It had all happened in a moment. He had heard the boobrie squawk in terror and come up from the bottom of the lake to see if he could help, and a man had shot something into his throat – a red hot needle it felt like . . . and then he remembered nothing more till he woke in a kind of snake pit in this ghastly place.

'I have failed my friends,' he thought, 'and I have failed myself.' And he felt so sad that he wanted to die.

From the rusty tank in the corner where the mermaids sat, came the sound of sobbing. Oona was sobbing because *men* kept coming down below to peer and pry – men that were worse even than Lord Brasenott – and she was terribly afraid. But the noisiest and most terrible tears came from Loreen.

'My baby!' she kept hiccuping. 'My little darling, where is he?'

183

When Sprott had overcome Art and broken open the door of the mermaid shed Walter had been asleep in his washing-up bowl and there had been no time for Loreen to grab him before she was thrown over Sprott's shoulder and carried towards the boat.

'Will someone find him?' gulped Loreen. And old Ursula said of course they would – but the trouble was, no one knew what was happening on the Island and who was left.

Perhaps the most heart-rending sight in that ghastly place were the boobrie chicks, penned in a wire cage, their yellow beaks bruised and blood-stained . . . and lying down, with her great yellow legs in the air like an outsize chicken ready for the pot, their mother. Lowering the struggling giant bird through the trapdoor had been so difficult that they had given her another injection and now the chicks climbed over her, peeping in bewilderment, not understanding why their mother was so still.

But Sprott's greatest prize was not in the hold. The kraken lay on the deck, tethered by ropes which bit so hard that he could not even turn his head, and every few minutes Sprott came up to look at him and rub his hands and gloat. He had no idea what it was that he had caught, only that it would make him very, very rich. For it could speak, this thing which they had caught when Des fell into its cave. It had said 'Father' once, when they nailed it down on to the deck, but now its eyes were closed and it spoke no more.

'Hurry up down there,' Sprott shouted to the crew who were fixing the starboard engine. They would have been gone long before but for the engine playing up. It was high time they got away across the Atlantic. He'd given orders to have the thing on the deck hosed down every ten minutes but it wasn't eating. None of the creatures were eating . . . they needed to be in proper cages.

For a moment he wondered if the little boy was dead – the one who'd tried to stop them in the cave. Probably not – the skulls of children were tougher than you'd think. All the same he'd be glad to be gone.

'I thought I told you to hurry,' Sprott shouted once again.

But still the *Hurricane* lay unmoving on the grey sea – and on her deck, the little kraken, his heart broken, prepared for death.

Minette sat on the floor of the boxroom, her hands round her knees, and waited for Fabio to wake.

She had been there for several hours and she would not move however much the aunts complained.

'You're not helping him,' said Etta. 'He'll come round when he's ready.'

But she did not speak in her usual brisk voice, and Minette took no notice. All the aunts were like wraiths since the kraken had gone.

So Minette watched and waited by her friend. Outside, in the bathroom, she could hear the high, stupid voices of Betty's children.

'There's something nasty in the washbasin. It smells fishy. You can't clean your teeth,' whined Boo-Boo.

'It's eaten my Tinkerbell toothpaste. I don't like it here. I want to go home!'

'I want to go home too. I want to go home *now*.'

Minette sighed. She could never get used to the awfulness of Boo-Boo and the Little One. What was in the washbasin was the merbaby, Walter. He was missing his mother, and chewed anything he could reach.

Fabio lay without moving on the bed; the bandage round his head stood out very white in the darkened room. What if he didn't come round at all?

But that was stupid. He was breathing. He had concussion, that was all.

Minette shut her eyes, remembering. They'd been in the cave, telling the kraken a story . . . trying to stop him going too near the entrance. Then suddenly something had hurtled down from the opening in the cliff above them and landed in the water. A man they had never seen before, gasping and struggling for breath.

They hadn't been frightened at first – not till he clambered out and stared at the kraken . . . stared and stared . . . Then he felt in his sodden clothes, and from an oilskin pouch he took out a whistle and blew three sharp shrill blasts.

They had understood then. Fabio charged at the man, trying to wrench the whistle away, but it was too late. More men came from the sea and the cave filled up with shouting and torchlight and the glint of weapons . . . Minette had gone to the kraken's head, slipping into the water with him, trying to calm him but the net came down over them both . . . He'd thought it was a game at first – cruelty was something he couldn't understand – and she'd half hoped they'd take her with him so that she could comfort him. But they had pulled her out roughly and thrown her back into the pool.

And as she climbed out she'd seen Fabio lying on the ledge of rock . . . and the blood seeping from his head . . .

Out in the corridor the Little One was whimpering again. 'They've given me the wrong sweeties. I've got blue sweeties and I'm a girl. Girls ought to have *pink* sweeties.'

It was another hour before Fabio stirred, but then he was awake at once.

'Have they got him? Has he gone?'

'Yes.'

Fabio put a hand to his head. 'Did they knock me out?'

'They kept thumping your head against the stone.' Minette's voice broke as she remembered Fabio's courage and the cruelty of the men.

'And the others? The stoorworm . . . the mermaids?'

'They've got everyone except Walter.'

Fabio had managed to sit up.

'Is the *Hurricane* still there?

'Yes. We don't know why but she is.'

'Then we must board her. We must rescue him. We must rescue everybody.'

Minette stared at him. 'You're mad. How could we? We've only got the *Peggoty* – and the aunts won't let us out of their sight. We're really prisoners now because they blame themselves for you being hurt and because they left the creatures unguarded to help Myrtle. You've no idea what it's like down there. And Dorothy broke one of the thug's noses with her wok; they dragged him back to the boat but there's blood everywhere.'

Fabio took no notice. 'We have to. We have to get to him.'

'Even if we did, what could we—' began Minette and broke off. She felt like Fabio underneath. They had to try and help.

Fabio had pushed back the bedclothes. The room spun round, then steadied. He was just trying his feet on the floor when the unspeakable Boo-Boo came in.

'That's my teddy you've got there. I put him to sleep in your bed when you were in the cave and I want him because we're going to play Mummies and Daddies in the garden and he's my little boy.'

Fabio threw the stuffed animal across the room.

'Get out,' he said. And then: 'There must be someone who could help.'

Minette looked at him. He had had an awful blow to his head – would he be able to cope with any more strangeness?

But that was silly. Fabio could cope with anything.

'There is somebody,' she said.

Herbert sat quietly on the point and looked out to the sea which until yesterday had been his home. He wore a pair of Art's trousers, stripy socks and a sweater of the Captain's. The clothes felt prickly on his skin, and his soul felt prickly too. The tears of Myrtle, the despair of the aunts, buzzed round his head. It had been so quiet in the sea.

But what was done was done. He was a man now, not a seal, and it was as a man that he must try to help the kraken's son.

The *Peggoty* was in the boathouse. She was only an old fishing boat, not a tenth the size of the *Hurricane*, but if he could get alongside and get a grappling hook on to the deck he could climb up the rope and board her. Some selkies, when they changed shape, had trouble with their arms and legs, but his were strong.

He was checking the *Peggoty*'s oars, when Fabio and Minette appeared in the doorway of the shed. Fabio had pulled a woollen cap over his bandage.

'We want to go with you,' said Minette.

Fabio was silent. He had expected to find it a shock meeting someone who not twenty-four hours ago had been a seal, but now nothing mattered except to get to the *Hurricane*. Herbert had been a handsome seal and he was a handsome man but what was important was that he looked trustworthy and reliable – and strong. Some people who listen to music on the cello can be a little arty and vague, but not Herbert.

'Have you asked the aunts?' said Herbert, coiling a rope.

The children did not answer. Then:

'We have to go. The kraken was our job. We have to help him, and the others too. We have to try.'

Herbert straightened himself and looked at them. He was a man now but he was not a man like other men. He had a sense of all nature being one . . . of children being part of the universe and not creatures set apart. He knew that if the little kraken died the sea would never be the same again, and he remembered that the kraken had trusted these two as he had trusted no one.

All the same, knowing the danger, he hesitated.

But it looked as though the matter would be taken out of his hands. For before he could speak all three of them heard the unmistakable drone of a helicopter coming towards the Island. The noise grew louder, the helicopter circled the Island once . . . then began the descent on to the level patch of grass behind the house.

Tears sprang to Minette's eyes and Fabio drew in a hissing breath. Now, just when they had a chance of reaching the kraken, they had been found and would be dragged back.

Frantically they looked about for somewhere to hide. But it was too late. A policeman was climbing out of the machine and hurrying towards the house; a policewoman followed.

The adventure was over.

Chapter Twenty

King's Cross Station had not looked so smart since the Queen had arrived there at the time of her silver jubilee.

There were streamers all over the station saying *Welcome Back!* and on Platform One where the train bringing the kidnapped children was due to arrive, was a party of schoolchildren carrying banners. The banners said things like *You are safe now* and *Your troubles are ended*, and the children who carried them had learnt a welcoming song which they would sing as soon as the snatched children stepped out of the train.

A chocolate firm had sent a bumper pack of sweets, and their prettiest salesgirl, dressed like a chocolate bar, was waiting to present it. A famous clothes shop had made up parcels of T-shirts, and a bicycle manufacturer had brought two mountain bikes to present to the children who had been snatched so cruelly by the kidnapping aunts. Everyone knew about the miracle which had made it possible for the police helicopter to swoop down and gather up the missing boy and girl in a single daring raid.

Mrs Danby, Minette's mother, was in the place of honour, standing on the strip of red carpet which had been put out for the children to walk on when they stepped out of their First Class Carriage. She wore a dazzling new outfit which she had bought with the money from the *Daily Screech*: a shocking pink suit and a little pillbox hat with a veil. When she ran forward to hug Minette she would push the veil up so that people could see her tears. Professor Danby stood beside her, looking solemn. Whenever his wife took a step forward so as to be nearer to where the train would stop, he took one too. He wasn't going to be upstaged by that show-off he'd been fool enough to marry!

The old Mountjoys had been given special chairs so that they could wait for their grandson in comfort. They were of course very pleased that Fabio had been found, but they couldn't help wondering if all the work they had put into making him into an English gentleman had been wasted. The children had been discovered on some rough island in the middle of the Atlantic ocean and that could hardly be a good thing. Maybe they would come off the train with straw in their hair and mud on their shoes – if they wore shoes at all.

And of course as well as the schoolchildren and the relatives and the Lady Mayoress with her golden chain, the platform was full of cameramen and journalists and television crews with all their gear. The moment when the poor, snatched, little children got down from the train and ran into the arms of their loved ones would be shown not just all over England but all over the world. Even now the commentators were setting the scene, babbling excitedly into their microphones.

'Only five minutes to go, before the train bringing

those frightened, wretched youngsters to safety will draw up just twenty metres from where I stand,' said the lady from ITV. 'Mrs Danby can hardly hold back her excitement – she has just run forward so as to get even closer to her missing daughter . . .'

This was true – Mrs Danby *had* run forward, but this was because her husband was up to his tricks again, trying to upstage her so that the camera picked him up as well as her and she wasn't having that.

'And the grandparents of the wild little boy who found shelter and kindliness in their home – what a touching couple they make, in the autumn of their years, waiting with joy for this great moment,' the commentator went on.

Up in Edinburgh, Professor Danby's housekeeper was glued to the telly. There'd be a row about which of the parents was to have the girl first, she thought, and hoped it would be the professor because she'd put flowers in Minette's room and polished her new writing desk.

Minette's mother's boyfriend was watching too, lying as usual with a can of lager on the sofa. He too hoped Minette would go to her father first. Not that he had anything against the kid but the flat was cramped and he'd got the sack again and needed somewhere to flake out in the day.

And in the hospital in Newcastle upon Tyne, Betty sat in the dayroom and watched, surrounded by other patients and those nurses who could spare a moment. She needed the treat because her hip was mending very slowly; she should have been out of hospital a week ago and there she still was.

'Only three more minutes now,' said one of the newscasters looking at the station clock, which was a silly thing to say. Since when have trains coming down from the North been on time, even trains full of police officers bringing kidnapped children back to safety?

The commentator described Mrs Danby's hat once more and told the viewers that old Mrs Mountjoy's face was full of longing.

The schoolchildren holding their banners shuffled their feet and cleared their throats, ready for their welcoming song.

The station clock ticked on.

And then at last they saw the train coming, curving round into the station, and a great cheer went up. The Lady Mayoress straightened her chain, the crowd that had gathered outside the platform gates waved, the television cameras whirred . . .

The train slowed down . . . stopped.

The door opened. A policewoman got down, and another . . . then they turned and held out their hands to the two children.

The girl was the first to come out. She was lifted down from the carriage and stood for a moment looking about her, smoothing down the velvet collar of her coat and patting her curls.

Then the boy was lifted down, and straightened his cap and dusted down his blazer.

'Where's my mummy?' said the little girl in a cross and whining voice. 'I want my mummy. You said you'd take us to her.'

'I want her too,' wailed the little boy. 'I want my mummy *now*.'

194

Mrs Danby's mouth fell open. The professor glared. 'Is this a joke?' snapped Mr Mountjoy.

And in the dayroom of the hospital in Newcastle upon Tyne, poor Betty gave a single high-pitched cry and fell back senseless in her chair.

Chapter Twenty-One

Herbert was magnificent. In spite of the darkness and the choppy sea he sent the *Peggoty* sailing steadily towards the single light burning on the *Hurricane*. His hands on the tiller never faltered, he seemed to understand the old boat as he understood the sea.

Fabio and Minette sat very close together in the stern, not daring to speak. When the helicopter took off again and they realized what a wonderful mistake had been made, they had wasted no more time. While Herbert was filling petrol cans by the jetty, they had climbed aboard and down into the little cabin full of fishing hooks and ropes and tackle and pulled a tarpaulin over their heads. With luck, by the time they were found, they would be too far out to turn back.

But it wasn't Herbert who found them – it was Aunt Etta and Aunt Coral. It had never occurred to the children that the aunts would be part of the boarding party. Dorothy was staying behind because she had sprained her wrist when she bashed Casimir with her wok and Herbert had forbidden Myrtle to come.

'You have had a shock, Myrtle, and you must rest,' Herbert had said, and that was that. But not even Herbert had been able to stop Etta and Coral.

They had never seen the aunts so angry.

'Turn back at *once*!' commanded Etta. 'These children will *not* face any more danger! I forbid it!' – and Coral tried to get hold of the tiller and force the boat to change course.

But Herbert stood firm. He had sensed the change in the sea and knew what would happen to the ocean if the kraken's son perished. Even the children did not matter compared to that.

They glided silently alongside the *Hurricane*. No lights were burning in the cabins; no one expected an attack. With unbelievable strength Herbert threw the knotted rope and they heard the grappling iron fasten on the wooden boards.

Within seconds, Herbert had climbed the rope and was on deck. Etta and the children followed. Coral with her bulk took longer but she did it.

They stood in silence, listening. Herbert had his knife ready. If they could cut the kraken free and push him overboard, he could swim to safety.

They had almost reached him when it happened.

The door from below opened, a beam of light was thrown on to the deck – and Lambert, in his pyjamas stood there, blinking.

The poor boy was definitely going crazy. Since the *Hurricane* had filled up with creepy-crawlies that weren't really there, Lambert had been plagued by dreadful dreams. In this one he'd dreamt that Old Ursula had come to his school, sliding on her tail, and said she was his grandmother and all the boys had jeered at him and thrown him buckets of fish.

Now he came on to the deck, too afraid to wake his father, and saw a huddle of shapes creeping towards the tarpaulin where the thing that didn't exist was lying.

He gave a cry of terror and as Herbert turned, the knife in his hand, the klaxons began to blare and searchlights raked the deck.

Ten minutes later, the rescuers had joined the prisoners in the stench and darkness of the hold.

You couldn't really blame the police. When the helicopter landed on the Island, two little children had run straight into the arms of the policewoman and begged to be taken home.

'Take us away,' they had lisped pathetically. 'We hate it here. Take us home to our mummy.'

It was clear that the poor little scraps had been abominably treated. They had not been allowed to clean their teeth and been given sweets which tasted nasty – drugged ones, the policewoman was sure. All the way they had whimpered and complained and it was clear that the aunts who had held them were as evil and dangerous as everyone imagined.

But of course the muddle took some time to sort out. The tax inspector had to come from Newcastle upon Tyne to fetch his children and no one knew whether the T-shirts and the chocolate bars should be given to them or kept for when the other children came. And the whole business of capturing the vile kidnappers and the children that they were holding had still to be done.

But it couldn't be done at once because a great fog had come down, covering the Western coast and making it impossible for helicopters to take off, or ships to move.

*

The prisoners had been in the hold of the *Hurricane* for several hours when they heard the engine judder into life.

Soon they would be off, and then . . . Nobody put into words what would happen once they were out in the Atlantic, but all of them knew. Why should Sprott let them live to tell the world what he had done.

In a corner, Minette was talking quietly to Fabio.

'If I could get to the kraken . . . just for a few minutes?'

Fabio shrugged. 'How would it help? We've nothing to cut him free with.'

'I've got an idea. It might not work, but we've got nothing to lose.'

'What sort of an idea?'

Minette looked round. The aunts were dozing, their backs against the wall; the worm was curled round himself like a piece of worn-out hosepipe . . .

She moved closer to Fabio and whispered in his ear.

Fabio looked doubtful. 'Remember what Aunt Etta said – that they can't do it till they're ready.'

'Yes, I know – but once or twice when he's been learning a song, I thought . . . And anything's better than nothing.'

'All right,' said Fabio. 'Let me think.'

He sat for a while with his head in his hands. Then he went over to speak to Herbert who nodded and went over to the mermaids' tank.

'I can't,' they heard poor Queenie say. 'I haven't the heart.'

But Herbert was firm: 'I'm afraid you must,' he said in his sensible voice.

An hour later Des came down the ladder with some bread and a bucketful of drinking water and as he did so, Queenie called to him.

'Des,' she trilled. 'Could you come here a minute?'

He put down his bucket and sidled past Herbert. He could never be sure whether this was or wasn't the man who had tried to strangle him on the point – it had been too dark to see his face – but Herbert gave him the creeps.

'I've got ever such a painful place here in my back,' Queenie went on. 'Would you come and look, please?'

Des bent over her and Queenie tossed her hair so that it fell over his face.

'No, not there,' she fluted. 'You show him, Oona.'

It was only thinking of the kraken that gave Oona the courage to come closer to the man with his horrible hot breath, but she did it, and she too tossed her long thick hair so that Des was completely covered in the mermaids' tresses.

'Where?' he kept saying. 'Where does it hurt?'

Only Boris was guarding the hatch – Casimir wasn't good for much since Dorothy had broken his nose – and Fabio now climbed up the ladder. 'Help,' he shouted. 'The mermaids are being pestered. Send someone down!'

Sprott heard him and was furious. He had forbidden the men to go near the twins.

'What's going on there?' he yelled and, as Boris turned, Fabio dodged round behind him running towards the deckhouse, while down below the mermaids began to scream.

200

The chase did not last long – Boris caught Fabio and almost threw him down into the hold. But Minette had been behind Fabio and managed to slip out unseen in the muddle and the fog, and make her way to where the captured kraken lay.

The kraken lay tethered and dangerously still. He still breathed but only just; his eyes were closed.

She tiptoed forward and laid her cheek against his head, and her tears fell on his face.

But Minette had not escaped from below deck to cry. She had only a few minutes to do what she had set herself to do.

'You mustn't give in like this,' she said into his ear. 'It's wrong. You're a brave and important person. You have to fight back.'

The kraken tried to turn his head but the ropes bit into his throat. She saw the look in his golden eyes and her heart sank. But she wouldn't seem to be sorry for him; that was not the way.

'You must remember who you are,' she said sternly.

The little kraken sniffed and was silent.

'You must think of your father,' she went on.

'Father,' said the kraken. He seemed a little stronger when he said that and she could see he was thinking of the mighty creature who had given him life.

'That's right.' Minette followed this up. 'What does your father do?'

The little kraken sighed. It was a heartbreaking sound, as though all the sorrow in the world was coming out of his throat.

'Go on. Think,' prompted Minette.

The kraken sighed again. He was not good at simply thinking. Then:

'Smiles,' he said.

'Yes. He smiles. He's got a lovely smile.' Minette saw the curve of the great beast's mouth as he swam into the bay. 'And what else does he do?'

There was another pause. Then: 'Swims,' said the little kraken. 'He swims.'

'That's right. He swims.' Minette nodded hard, giving encouragement. 'And what does he do when he swims?'

No answer.

'What does he do when he swims round the oceans of the world making everything better? Think.'

The little kraken thought. You could see him trying, but the ropes were beginning to cut into his flesh. He was too young to think through pain.

'Don't know,' he moaned.

But Minette would give him no chance to go under. 'Yes, you do. When he swims he does something else. What is it?'

Another sigh. Then: 'He hums,' said the little kraken.

'That's right.' She rubbed his head to give him encouragement. 'He hums, doesn't he? Humming is what krakens *do*.'

He tried to turn his head. His eyes were still bewildered.

'Humming is what krakens do,' repeated Minette. 'Isn't it?'

'Yes.' His voice was very weak but he was following her.

'And you're a kraken,' she insisted. 'Aren't you? A kraken is what you are.'

It didn't seem as though the poor exhausted creature could speak again, but he took a weary breath and tried once more.

'I'm a kraken,' he repeated obediently. 'A kraken is what I *am*.'

At first she'd thought it was going to work. There had been a flash of pride in his eyes as he spoke; but almost at once he fell silent and turned away – and then Boris came and pushed her roughly down the ladder.

Now she sat beside Fabio, her head in her hands and knew that it was over. She had done all she could and she had failed.

In the darkness, the wan faces of the captives showed a wretchedness that was beyond tears. The two aunts sat with closed eyes trying to bear what they had done. Facing their own deaths was not so hard but what they had done to Fabio and Minette was not to be endured. Only Herbert was still upright, listening to the sound of the water against the sides of the ship.

Another hour passed . . . and another . . . The *Hurricane*'s engine had been turned off while they waited for the fog to lift, but now they heard it start up again.

Unsteady at first, fainter than before . . . wavering . . . but gradually settling into a kind of thrumming rhythm.

Except that the engine hadn't sounded quite like that . . .

Fabio who had been dozing, sat up suddenly and dug Minette in the ribs.

Then slowly, wonderingly, the wretched prisoners looked at each other with a dawning hope.

The great kraken had reached the Islands of the Southern Reef. The turquoise water, the coral strands, were staggeringly beautiful.

There was little to do in this paradise. The people who lived there respected the sea and the creatures in it, and they came out to pay their respects to the great kraken, standing with bowed heads. They did not gawp or gape or stare; the legend of the kraken who healed the sea was in their stories and had been for generations.

'He does not smile,' said the old chief, whose great-grandmother had seen the kraken when he came before and told him about the healer's mouth curving in a bow which made everyone joyous to watch.

'He is troubled,' said the chief's wife, who was a magic woman.

'How strangely his hum is sounding,' said a child. 'There are two hums, aren't there? A big hum and a little hum.'

'It must be an echo.'

But the kraken had stopped swimming. He was quite still in the water, resting. His head was tilted. Like the islanders he was listening . . . listening . . .

What was going on? His own hum was being interfered with. It was being disturbed. This had never happened before. Sometimes there had been an echo from his hum when he swam in a fjord between mountains, and sometimes the whales joined in, but this was different. What he could hear was his own hum but it was smaller.

He fell silent, and all the creatures under the water came up to look at him and wonder what was happening.

But the silence was not complete. The small hum, the *underneath* hum, was still there. It was unsteady, quavery . . . but it was growing now in strength.

A great judder went through the kraken, sending the resting birds up in a flutter from his back. He made himself absolutely quiet once more, but it was still there – this other fainter hum that wasn't his own hum . . . and yet was just exactly that.

Then the people on the barrier reef saw a most extraordinary sight. The great kraken reared up out of the water – and now he did not hum. Instead he roared.

And then he turned.

Chapter Twenty-Two

'I don't want to watch! I don't *want* to!' shrieked Lambert. He tried to hold on to the cabin door but his father dragged him out so roughly that he fell forward on to the deck.

'You *will* watch, you namby-pamby little shirker. You'll watch them go overboard and you'll like it. It's time you learnt that you don't get something for nothing.'

Pushing and pulling, kicking Lambert's shins, Mr Sprott forced his son towards the rail.

He felt hard done by. If the aunts had sold him the island as he wanted he wouldn't have to drown them now, and the children too. It was their own fault really. There was no way he could get his money-making schemes under way with people blathering and giving the game away. He was going to say that he'd found the creatures wild at sea and rescued them.

'Right, go and get them,' he ordered Des. And then, furiously, 'I thought I told you to stop the thing making that blasted noise!'

Des looked at the kraken, still tethered to the deck.

'I've tried, boss. I've kicked him and I've thumped him but you said I wasn't to do him in.'

Evil people cannot bear the sound of the hum. They feel it as a threat to all they stand for, and the

206

kraken had been humming now for many hours.

Boris meanwhile had opened the hatch.

'Out,' he said. 'Up! Only the peoples.'

One by one they came out. Fabio, Minette, the aunts . . . Herbert.

On deck it was cold but marvellously fresh after the stuffiness of the hold. Gulls were flying above them; it all looked so normal – except for the look in Sprott's eyes.

'I don't want to see them drown, I don't want to,' yelled Lambert, twisting in his father's grasp.

The children moved closer together. It was going to happen, then – and almost straight away.

Boris and Des had fetched the weights they were going to tie to their victims' ankles; not that there was much chance that they would be able to swim to safety. The *Hurricane* had been steaming steadily away from the Island.

The aunts had come to stand behind the children; Etta behind Minette, Coral behind Fabio as though by some miracle they could still protect them.

Fabio and Minette had linked hands. Everything inside them seemed to have turned to stone.

Don't let me make a fuss, Fabio was praying. Don't let me be like Lambert.

'We'll start with the fat one,' ordered Sprott. 'Take her to the rails and get the weights on.'

Des went over to Aunt Coral.

'Move,' he said, prodding her with the butt of his gun – and as he did so, Fabio went mad.

'How dare you!' he shouted and tried to attack the bodyguard with his fists.

Sprott thought this was very funny. 'All right, you

207

can go first then if you're so full of beans,' he said, and the two thugs pinned Fabio's arms behind his back and started to carry him to the side.

They were trying to fix weights on to his thrashing legs when the skipper put his head out of the wheelhouse.

'Better hurry,' he said. 'I don't like the look of the sky.'

There was nothing to like the look of. Not the sea, not the sky, not the surface of the water, not the clouds. Some dreadful weather was on the way.

The waves darkened, the water boiled; the sun vanished behind a mushroom cloud.

The gulls flew up screeching.

And on the deck of the *Hurricane* – someone began to scream.

'Hold on to me,' Fabio had shouted to Minette, but they were torn apart at once by the mountainous icy waves.

Minette had thought of herself as a good swimmer but this was nothing to do with swimming – she was being hurled up, then sucked down, rolled over . . .

And the cold was beyond belief.

All round her were broken planks and debris from the *Hurricane*. The ship had split in two the instant the great kraken had rammed her. She saw the roof of the boobrie's splintered cage bobbing close by; two of the chicks were clinging to the top of it – but where was the third?

A wave broke over her head and she went under again; the weight of the water pressed her down and down; her lungs were bursting. I'm going to die, she thought, as far as she could think at all.

Then with a last thrust of her legs she reached the surface. And as she did so, she saw someone quite close to her, swimming as masterfully and strongly as if he was in a millpond rather than the raging sea.

'Wait, I'm coming,' called Herbert, and she reached out for him, but then another wave took her and she went under yet again and was sure she was lost. Then she felt herself pulled up and up by her hair . . . and found that she was clinging on to Herbert's back and able to breathe once more.

'Hold on tight, but don't choke me,' called Herbert – and set off through the waves as calmly as he had done when he was still a seal.

'Fabio?' she managed to ask.

But Herbert had not seen Fabio.

They passed the stoorworm and saw something large gripped tightly in the coils of his tail. The worm's ancestors had come from the sea and Herbert wasted no time on him. He would get Aunt Coral to safety if anybody could.

A mattress swam past them, then the galley table with the third boobrie chick clinging on by his yellow feet.

'Keep still, Aunt Etta,' came Queenie's high-pitched voice above the sound of the waves. 'You mustn't wriggle.'

The twins were holding Aunt Etta up between them as she spluttered and kicked her feet.

Hanging on to Herbert's back took all Minette's strength, but she was still searching desperately for Fabio.

'Please, Herbert, we must find him.'

After he and Minette were torn apart, Fabio had sighted the lifeboat which had been thrown clear when the *Hurricane* sank. He managed to swim towards it . . . to get a hand on the gunnel . . . If the people inside it would help him he could pull himself up.

But the people inside it were Stanley Sprott and his crew.

Sprott looked over the side and saw the struggling boy. 'Get rid of him,' he said.

And as the small hand came up, Boris hit it with an oar and pushed the boy back into the water.

There was not much hope for Fabio after that. He was going down for the last time when Herbert found him.

'Hold on to my shoulder,' he ordered. 'And don't talk.'

Herbert was an amazing swimmer but he knew that to support two children all the long way back to the Island might be beyond his strength. Even a seal would not try to swim with two pups on his back.

Everyone was in difficulties. The raft on which the boobrie chicks balanced was sinking and above them the boobrie mother squawked in anguish, not knowing which of the two to pick up in her beak. The worm's tail muscles had gone into cramp from holding up the waterlogged Aunt Coral . . .

Herbert measured the long way to the Island and set his teeth.

'Come on, everybody, follow me,' he called manfully.

One could only do one's best.

*

The kraken had found his son. He cared for nothing else. He swam away from the shipwreck with the child on his back. Anger still coursed through his body. He was not the Healer of the Sea now. He was a father whose child had been hurt. Let everyone else beware for he and his son were on their way!

But after the first joy of being safe, the little kraken wriggled forward so that his mouth was right against his father's ear, and began to talk very fast in Polar. He was explaining what had happened and how the people on the Island had tried to keep him safe.

And then he said the word which the great kraken had spoken when he first swam into the bay.

'Children?' said the little kraken. And again, looking back at the wreckage: 'Children?'

But it was not really a question. It was an order. The little kraken was growing up.

And the great kraken sighed because he wanted above all to be away from the shrieks and the splintered wood of the wreckage and be in the quietness of the sea. But he heeded his son – and he turned and swam back to the wreck and to the struggling creatures trying to hold each other up in the water.

Then Minette and Fabio felt something below them . . . the strong living island of muscle that was the kraken's back . . . and felt it rise and rise till everyone was safely gathered on it – the aunts and the creatures, the boobries in their cage . . . and they themselves, sliding off Herbert's weary shoulders to feel firm ground beneath their feet.

It was an incredible, magic journey that they took after the panic and terror they had been through – floating secure and safe on the great creature's back, until the Island was in sight, and there was no more danger and no more fear.

But the kraken had not saved everybody.

Stanley Sprott lay sprawled across the bottom of the battered, leaking lifeboat. Boris, only half conscious, was clinging to the gunnel. Des was hanging over the side, trying to be sick; he had been drinking seawater. Lambert was curled up like a baby between the skipper and the mate.

Casimir had drowned in the struggle to reach the lifeboat after the *Hurricane* was rammed.

They had been drifting for a long time. The sea was still strange; slate colour one minute; the colour of blood the next. No rescue ships were setting out in this awesome ocean.

In the lifeboat there was no more water and no more food. The men's lips were blistered. Their swollen tongues stuck to the roof of their mouths. Befuddled as they were, they tried to make sense of what had happened.

Only they couldn't. No one could make sense of it.

'An island?' muttered Sprott. He could see it, bigger than anyone could believe, moving towards them with the speed of a comet.

But how could it? How could an island move?

'It wasn't there,' said Lambert suddenly. Weakened by hunger and thirst, those were the only words he could still say.

Sprott's head was a jumble of pictures.

A mermaid holding up . . . an aunt. But had there really been mermaids? And a great bird the size of an elephant flapping over the wreckage . . .

No, it was ridiculous. It was impossible. He fingered the bruise on his forehead. He must have concussion.

'Not . . . really there . . .' murmured Lambert. He wouldn't last much longer unless they were rescued soon.

I'm going mad, thought Sprott. I'll have to be careful. We'll all have to be careful or they'll put us in a loony bin if we're rescued. All that happened was that a storm came up and the *Hurricane* was wrecked. Everything else is nonsense.

'Not . . . there . . .' said Lambert faintly.

Sprott looked at his son. He had always despised Lambert but he was sorry now. Lambert was right. He had said all along that the . . . things . . . weren't really there and they weren't. How could they have been?

'Quite right, Lambert,' said Stanley Sprott, and leant back and closed his eyes.

If they were rescued he'd say nothing – and see that the others said nothing too. He wasn't going to be locked up as a loony, that was for sure . . .

The last days on the Island were strangely happy. The children knew they would soon be fetched away but they were able to enjoy each moment as it came and being in an adventure seemed to have done everybody good.

The stoorworm no longer complained about being too long for his thoughts.

213

'If I'd been any shorter I couldn't have held up Aunt Coral in the sea,' he said and stopped talking about plastic surgery once and for all.

As for Loreen, when Aunt Myrtle fetched Walter out of the washbasin and put him in his mother's arms she let out a shriek of joy.

'He's grown hair!' she cried.

'He's grown *a* hair,' said Queenie who was giving herself airs because she had saved Aunt Etta.

But the most exciting thing happened to the boobrie. After she waddled up to her nest with her three bedraggled chicks she found somebody sitting in it.

The boobrie paused, hissed . . . stretched out her neck. Who was it who *dared* to sit on *her* nest? Hooting, honking and complaining, she flapped her wings and prepared to attack.

Then suddenly she stopped. She lay down in front of the stranger, she clapped her beak against his . . . her eyes rolled with welcome and with love.

'My goodness,' said Fabio. 'It's her husband. He's come back!'

And he had. He didn't seem to be a very intelligent bird but knowing that there were two boobries now to look after the chicks was a great relief to everybody.

Herbert was of course a hero, but not at all conceited. He began straight away to tidy up the aunts' house and to label Art's storage jars and to show him how to cut the heads off fish.

But it was Myrtle who had been his special friend and he did everything he could to help her. He told her when her skirt was on back to front and he

214

corrected her when she played a tune too fast on the cello, and he insisted that she had swimming lessons twice a day.

'Oh, Herbert, the water is so cold!' Myrtle would cry.

But Herbert said it was dangerous to live so close to the sea and not be able to swim, and every morning and every evening Myrtle had to get her rubber ring and put on her chill-proof vest and Aunt Etta's navy-blue bloomers and go into the sea.

But the important thing – the thing that was on everybody's mind – was what was going to happen to the kraken.

After he had brought them safely to the shore the great kraken had moved a little way away to the mouth of the bay. He stayed submerged most of the time and out of sight and his son stayed with him.

'He's thinking,' said Aunt Etta and she was right.

He was thinking about what to do next. Should he give up his healing journey around the world and go back to the Arctic? Or should he find somewhere else to leave his son? For he knew without being told that things were going to be different on the Island.

Then one morning Ethelgonda appeared, shimmering above her tombstone, so they knew that it would be an important day.

And sure enough by noon the great kraken swam slowly into the bay with his son on his back. It was a most anxious moment. No one could blame the kraken if he turned his back on human beings once again and left the sea to spoil, and it was as though all those who waited by the shore were holding their breath.

Then he began to talk. He talked in Polar and it was his son who translated.

'Although people deserve that I should leave them to their mess and their wickedness, I have decided to go on with my journey around the oceans of the world. But I shall not take one year and one day to make the journey. I shall take two years and two days . . . or even three years and three days, so that my son, who has been restored to me, can come also and be with me at my side.'

When he said that a great cheer went up and Fabio and Minette hugged each other because it was the closest to a happy ending they could hope for.

That evening when it was quiet, the little kraken came and said goodbye all by himself to the children who had cared for him. There was just one bun left in the boobrie tin but when Fabio gave it to the kraken he did not at once open his mouth. He said: '*Share!*'

So the children broke the bun into three parts and everybody had a piece. It was a most squashed and sorry-looking bun, with cracked icing and a wilting Smartie clinging to the top . . . but afterwards the children remembered it as tasting like a bun in Paradise.

The next morning the kraken and his son had gone.

And only a few hours later the noise they had been expecting was heard over the Island: the sound of a helicopter. But not one . . . three . . . and coming from them a whole posse of policemen with guns and handcuffs and body-armour – come to fetch back the children and arrest the aunts.

Chapter Twenty-Three

Aunt Etta and Aunt Coral had been in prison for several weeks before their trial for kidnapping came to the courts. The children were not allowed to visit them and so the first time they saw them was in the dock at the Old Bailey, handcuffed to the police-women who brought them up from the cells.

For Minette and Fabio, seeing them like that was like being kicked very hard in the stomach and Minette gave a gasp of distress which the people in the courtroom heard.

'Poor little thing – look how frightened she is,' they whispered – and it was true. Minette was very frightened and so was Fabio – frightened for the aunts and what might happen to them; very frightened indeed.

Etta had always been thin but now she was all bone, and Coral's bulk had gone so that her skin hung in folds. It wasn't the prison food or the other prisoners that had worn them down, it was waking up day after day to the grey walls which closed them in. It was their loss of freedom.

The courtroom was very dark and very old. The judge sat high above everyone else like God, and below him were men in gowns and wigs: a ferrety-looking man who was the prosecuting counsel and had to prove that the aunts were guilty, and a man with a round face like a Christmas pudding who was the defence counsel and had to try and show that the aunts were innocent. The jury – three women and nine men, sat on the judge's right. One of them, a lady with a large bosom and red hair, kept fanning herself with a piece of paper. Minette's parents sat on benches facing the judge, as far away from each other as possible, and the old Mountjoys were in the back row.

It was only Aunt Etta and Aunt Coral who were being tried. Myrtle had been allowed to return to the Island because Mr Sprott was in a clinic in America and too muddled to accuse anyone of kidnapping his son. Etta and Coral were glad of that. They thought that Myrtle would probably have died in prison.

The case had attracted a lot of attention. *Killer Aunts Brought to Justice* screamed the newspaper headlines and the strange pictures of Etta and Coral that had been on the walls of the police station were printed again, making everyone certain that these were the most evil women in the world.

'Will the prisoner stand,' said the clerk of the court – and the children drew in their breath for the prisoner was Etta.

The charge was read out.

'Do you plead guilty or not guilty?' she was asked.

'Not guilty,' said Etta, holding her head high.

Then the witnesses were called. Minette's mother came first, tripping towards the witness box and patting her hair. She was sorry the trial wasn't shown on the telly because her hat was exactly right – serious and dark but very flattering – and because she had been an actress she swore to tell the whole truth and nothing but the truth in a very dramatic way.

'Is this the woman who met you at King's Cross Station?' asked the prosecuting counsel who looked like a ferret, pointing at Etta.

'Yes it is.'

'And did you think she was a fit person to have charge of your daughter?'

'Yes, I did, because she came from an agency. But I thought she had a sinister face.'

'Could you tell us what you mean by sinister . . . ?'

Minette's father was called next and described the false message he had had to say that Minette would not be travelling to Edinburgh.

Then it was Minette's turn.

There had been a lot of argument about whether Fabio and Minette were old enough to give evidence, but in the end it was decided that they could. So Minette too swore to tell the whole truth and nothing but the truth and then a footstool was fetched so that her head came over the edge of the witness box and the ferrety man began.

'Now, Minette, will you tell us what happened when you travelled with this person to Edinburgh,' he said. 'Just take your time,' he said, speaking very carefully, as though Minette was three years old.

'We talked about things,' said Minette.

'What sort of things?'

'Seals . . . and whether there were ghosts or not . . . and then I asked her if there was a third place.'

'Could you tell us what you mean by that?'

Minette bent her head, thinking. 'All my life I've

kept going backwards and forwards between my parents . . . and when I got there they were always horrible about each other so I got . . . tired. And sad. And I asked Aunt Etta if there was a third place. A place that wasn't *either* or *or* – and she said there was, there was one for everybody. Only they had to be brave and want it.'

'And what happened then?'

'I fell asleep. And when I woke up I was there. In the third place.'

'I see. You woke up in a completely strange place. And were you frightened?'

Minette smiled – a slow, very sweet smile which lit up the dark courtroom like a beacon. 'No. Not for long. I had a nightlight you see. I was frightened in London and in Edinburgh because of the dark and the cracks in the ceiling. I used to think I saw tigers . . . and my parents both thought I was silly. But there when I woke, the first thing I saw was this light.'

The ferrety man in the wig didn't like her answer. His job was to prove how wicked the aunts were and she wasn't helping. 'Are you telling me that you woke up in a completely strange place *having been kidnapped* and you weren't frightened?'

Minette lifted her chin.

'I wasn't kidnapped,' she said clearly. 'I was *chosen*.'

That evening the newspapers quoted her words. '*I wasn't kidnapped, I was chosen,*' *says child snatch victim*, and they all carried pictures of Minette.

The next morning it was Aunt Coral's turn and it was Fabio who went into the witness box and climbed on to the footstool. Again it was the ferrety prosecutor who asked the first questions.

'Now, my boy, will you tell us what happened on the way to Greymarsh Towers.'

'I was sick,' said Fabio.

'Is that because you were frightened?'

'Yes.'

'You were frightened of that lady there?' he asked, pointing to Aunt Coral.

'No. I was frightened of going back to school. It was a horrible place. They put my head down the toilet and kicked me and hung me out of the top-floor windows by my ankles because I came from Brazil and wasn't like them.'

There was a sympathetic murmur from the public gallery and the lady with orange hair stopped fanning herself and made a clucking noise.

'I don't think we need to hear about your school,' said the ferret, but the judge leant down and said Fabio should tell his story in his own way.

'So Aunt Coral went to talk to the matron and then she came back and said I couldn't go to school because they were in quarantine and I was terribly pleased. But then I realized it meant going back to my grandparents and that was almost as bad. They made me kneel on dried peas and they kept saying how vulgar my mother was. And then I realized that Aunt Coral knew how I felt because she was rather a magic person and I knew I could trust her.'

'So you were drugged and kidnapped,' the prosecutor went on.

Minette at this point had smiled but Fabio didn't. He glared, but the words he said were the same.

'I wasn't kidnapped,' he said. 'I was *chosen*.'

By the next day the newspapers were writing rather differently about the trial and some strange things were happening. Those children who were old enough to hear about the trial began to ask their parents for different bedtime stories: stories about magical aunts who came and took children away to islands where they didn't have to go to school.

Of course the aunts were guilty, everyone knew that. They would go to prison, probably for the rest of their lives, but there wasn't so much glee about, and the people who stood outside the courtroom holding up banners saying *Hanging is too good for them* stopped yelling and went home.

The third day of the trial was the last and the ferret started his questions again.

'What exactly did you do on the Island?' he wanted to know.

'We worked,' said the children. 'We helped to clean out the animals and milk the goats and feed the baby seals.'

'Exactly. You worked all the time? From dawn to dusk.'

'Yes.'

'And didn't you get tired?

'Of course we got tired.' Fabio scowled at him. 'What's wrong with being tired? Working like that was *good*. Everybody ought to do it instead of messing about at school trying to solve maths problems that don't have anything to do with real life and writing silly essays about people who are dead.'

When he found he couldn't drive the children into a corner, the ferret started on the aunts and it seemed as though there really couldn't be any hope. They *had* taken the children without their parents' knowledge; they didn't try to deny that. Neither Coral nor Etta were any good at telling lies.

And now it came to the end, to the summing-up, when the judge had to make the jury understand exactly what the case was about. Everyone in the court was silent, everyone knew the verdict would be guilty, but even those people who had wanted it at the beginning weren't so certain now.

Then Etta beckoned to the Christmas pudding man who was supposed to be defending them and whispered something, and he went over to the judge and whispered to him, and the judge nodded. No one knew what had been said but after a few minutes a clerk came in carrying two big dictionaries.

'Your honour,' said the pudding. 'I ask for leave to read out the two most up-to-date definitions of kidnapping. The first comes from the London Dictionary and it says: *Kidnap: To hold a person against their will.*' He turned to Minette. 'May I ask you to step into the box again.'

She did so.

'Would you say you had been held against your will?'

'*No,*' said Minette.

The question was repeated to Fabio.

'*No,*' shouted the boy.

The pudding picked up the second book. 'The definition of kidnapping given here is: *To hold a person for ransom. To demand money to secure the victim's release.*'

He looked at the benches where Minette's parents

223

and Fabio's grandparents were sitting. Then he called them out one by one, and to each of them he said: 'Have you ever been asked for a single penny by either of these ladies?'

And crossly, peevishly, they admitted that they had not.

'In that case, your honour, it is my opinion that no kidnap took place.'

The jury were out for six hours and during the whole of this time Fabio and Minette absolutely refused to leave the building.

'We're staying till they bring in the verdict,' said Fabio – and nothing the police or the social workers or anyone else could say would move them.

So they sat on hard chairs in an office behind the courtroom and waited. They were so tired they could hardly stop themselves from slipping to the ground but they did it. It was like keeping watch when someone was ill or dying; it had to be done.

It was after midnight before the jury returned and everybody filed back into the courtroom.

'Have you reached a verdict?' asked the judge, leaning down from his box.

'We have, my lord,' replied the foreman in a solemn voice.

'And do you find the defendants guilty or not guilty?'

There had never been such silence. Not a breath was heard in the court; not a rustle . . .

The foreman raised his head.

'Not guilty.'

Oddly it was not Minette but Fabio who burst into tears.

Chapter Twenty-Four

The Island had never looked more beautiful. The sea sparkled and danced, the sun shone through the green crests on the waves; and on the hill the blossoming gorse was a mass of gold.

The children had been allowed to come up for a week to say goodbye. Minette had to go back to her parents, but Fabio's mother was taking him back to South America. She had read about the trial and about Fabio's school and she no longer thought that her son needed to grow up as an English gentleman.

So it should have been a really sad farewell, but it wasn't because the aunts had called them into the dining room the day they came and shown them an important-looking document covered in red seals.

'It's our will,' they said.

The children started to read it but they couldn't make head nor tail of it and in the end Etta said: 'What it says is that we have left you the Island. To both of you jointly. When we die the Island will be yours.'

They had stood round them; all the aunts – Etta and Coral and Myrtle and Dorothy – and nodded in a pleased way.

'We know that you will regard it as a Sacred Trust,' they said.

The children could hardly believe it at first. It was

too big to take in: the thought that the Island would one day be theirs, and they could live on it and care for it, and be together. It made the years in between seem unimportant. Minette was not so frightened now of her parents' moods – and they were trying to behave better. Time would go quickly – very soon now she and Fabio would return and their real lives would begin.

'Will you manage the work till we come back?' Fabio asked and they said, yes they would because Dorothy had decided to stay. She thought it was time to hang up her wok and she had decided to breed piranha fish in a tank so that if any more Sprotts came to the Island she could see them off.

As for Herbert, he went on making himself useful as he had done ever since they escaped from the *Hurricane*. He polished the napkin rings and tidied Art's cutlery drawer and ordered some bedroom slippers for the Sybil from a catalogue.

But most of all he went on helping Myrtle. He showed her how to keep her hair tidy in a net, he stuck her loose sheet music together with Sellotape and every single morning and every single evening he saw that she put on Aunt Etta's bloomers and her rubber ring and had her swimming lesson in the sea.

All the same, Fabio and Minette, who had not seen him since before the trial, felt that Herbert had changed. He seemed to be working too hard, as though he was afraid of what might happen if he did not keep busy, and sometimes they caught him gazing out of the window with a strange look in his large brown eyes.

'He's homesick,' Myrtle whispered to the children. 'He misses the sea.'

The children were very upset. Herbert, after all, had saved their lives.

'Isn't there anything that can be done?' asked Fabio.

Aunt Myrtle sighed. 'He *could* be turned back into a seal,' she said slowly. 'There is a way.'

'Not a knife?' said Minette, horrified.

'No. That might work but . . .' She shook her head. 'The mermaids say that if one weeps seven tears over a selkie when the moon is rising . . . Seven human tears . . .'

'But could you bear it?' asked Minette. 'I mean, he's your friend.'

Myrtle looked down at her Wellington boots. 'I could . . . bear it,' she said, biting her lip, 'if it is the right thing to do. One can always bear what is right.'

So they went to the other aunts and had a meeting and then they went to find Herbert who was cleaning the windows of the sitting room.

'Herbert, we want you to tell us the truth,' said Aunt Etta. 'Were you happier as a seal? Do you want to return?'

Herbert spun round, the polishing cloth in his hand. There was no need for him to answer. They only had to look into his eyes.

'He has reached the Rock of the Farnes,' Herbert said in a dreamy voice. 'But he swims slowly. I could catch him up.'

So then they realized that Herbert's thoughts all this time had been with the great kraken and that he longed to swim with him and be his escort in the work of cleaning the sea.

But when they told Herbert what the mermaids had said and that he could be turned into a seal again if someone wept seven human tears over him he shook his head.

'Myrtle stayed by my side when my mother died; she played music to me in all weathers. I couldn't leave her now.'

So then Myrtle stepped forward and now she was not a vague and dippy woman whose hair fell down. She was a heroine.

'If it is right for you to swim with the great kraken you must do so, Herbert,' she said and though there was a sob in her throat she held her head high.

They decided to do the turning in the crystal cave and of course everyone wanted to come. The Captain couldn't leave his bed but the stoorworm promised to tell him all about it and the mermaids insisted on being there, and the naak and even the boobries, though it wasn't at all certain that they knew what was going on.

They had to wait until the moon broke out of its covering of cloud – but when Herbert threw off his dressing gown and stood there only in Art's boxer shorts, everyone sighed because it was all so dignified and beautiful, like a ceremony in ancient Greece.

It was Myrtle of course who was to do the actual crying, and because the tears had to fall directly on his head, Herbert knelt before her . . . and then she began.

She remembered all the good times – the music on Seal Point, the silent evenings beside her friend watching the sunset . . .

One tear fell on Herbert's head . . . then two . . . then three . . . four . . . five . . . six . . .

Only one more.

But just when everyone was clutching everyone else ready for the great moment, the tears stopped.

It was most embarrassing. Myrtle sniffed. She blinked, she blushed. She had shed six tears; and she couldn't shed a seventh.

For the truth was (though she never told anyone) that at that moment she had suddenly realized that she need never again go into the cold sea in her chill-proof vest and her sister's navy bloomers. She still minded terribly losing Herbert – but the relief had blocked her tear ducts as thoroughly as if they had been plugged with cement.

It was a dreadful moment, but of course help was at hand. Minette only had to think of saying goodbye to the man who had saved her life and she was off.

She took Myrtle's place – and as the seventh tear fell on to Herbert's head there was a flash of blinding jagged light.

And when they looked again they knew they had done right. On the ledge of rock was a pair of crumpled boxer shorts – but streaking out of the cave into the open sea was a silver hunk of streamlined muscle which thrust through the waves like an arrow.

The next morning was the children's last on the Island and they got up early and walked along the strand as they had done on the first day when they woke up to find they had been kidnapped.

'You will come back, won't you?' Minette asked.

'You won't stay and become Prime Minister of Brazil?'

She wanted to make him swear; to have a kind of ceremony – but then she saw his face as he looked out over the Island and saw that he loved it as she did, and she knew for certain that they would both be back. And the ache of parting became a different sort of ache – an ache of happiness – and then they turned and went back towards the house where the aunts were waiting.

Turn the page for an extract from

MOUNTWOOD
SCHOOL
for
Ghosts

by exciting new storytelling talent
TOBY IBBOTSON

Based on an original idea by his mother, the late, great
EVA IBBOTSON

Percy

The next day when Daniel came home from school, his new neighbours had arrived. They were called Mr and Mrs Bosse-Lynch, and Daniel's Great-Aunt Joyce, who had been spying from her window all day, was very satisfied. They had the right sort of car, and the right sort of clothes, and Mr Bosse-Lynch had started trimming the hedge immediately. Then two ladies from the town had arrived to clean the house, and Great-Aunt Joyce had heard Mrs Bosse-Lynch telling them what to do before they had even got through the door.

That night, when Daniel had put his light out and lay in the darkness waiting for sleep, he heard something. At first he thought that it must be a pigeon under the slates. But it wasn't the right cooing and scratching noise that pigeons made. It seemed to be coming from the wall beside his bed. On the other side of the wall, he knew, was an attic room just like his in the house next door. The noise was more a snuffling or gulping kind of noise. He sat up and put his ear to the wall. Now he could hear quite clearly. He heard stifled sobs, and sniffs. Someone was crying.

Daniel lay down again and tried to think. Perhaps Mrs Bosse-Lynch was secretly a very tragic person, with a horrible sad secret that she crept up to the attic and cried about at night. He hoped not, because he didn't want to feel sorry for someone whom horrid Great-Aunt Joyce approved of. But it was far more likely that they had a prisoner in the attic. They had kidnapped someone, probably a rich man's daughter, and sneaked her into the house. Soon they would cut off her ear and send it to the desperate parents. On the other hand, it could be a poor mad relation whom they didn't want anybody to know about. Daniel's friend Charlotte had read a book about someone like that. It was called *Jane Eyre* and was one of her absolute favourites.

Either way, Daniel had to make contact. He sat up again and knocked three times on the wall. The sniffling stopped.

'Hello, who's there?' he called. 'Do you need help?'

Still there was no sound. But then part of the wall slowly went soft and bulgy. The bulge got bigger, and separated itself from the wall. It was swirly and colourless, almost transparent. Then parts of it started taking shape, a hand appeared here, a leg there. The air in the room was suddenly icy cold, and in front of Daniel stood a small boy in a nightshirt,

4

with golden curls and big weepy eyes.

'You are a ghost, aren't you?' said Daniel. 'I thought you were someone in trouble.'

'I am someone in trouble,' said the ghost, and huge ghostly tears started to roll down its cheeks. 'I am someone in terrible trouble.'

'I think I saw when you came,' said Daniel. 'You were in the removal van.'

'Yes, I was,' said the ghost. 'It wasn't a bus.' The tears rolled ever faster down its pale cheeks.

'Of course it wasn't a bus, it was a removal van.'

'But I thought it was,' gulped the ghost. 'And I don't know where I am and I don't know where Father and Mother are and—'

'Please try to stop crying,' said Daniel. 'And keep your voice down or you'll wake Great-Aunt Joyce.'

The ghost was obviously a young child, and seemed to be working himself into hysterics. 'If you calm down and tell me about it, I might be able to help.'

Daniel was secretly a bit disappointed. Ever since the arrival of the removal van he had been hoping for something really shockingly ghastly, perhaps a leering headless skeleton or a viciously grinning ghost murderer who dissolved his victims in acid. Anything really that would scare Great-Aunt Joyce to death, or at least make her flee from Markham Street and never return. But if she came up now and saw this weeping boy, she would probably just slap him and shoo him out.

However, even a small sad ghost is better than no ghost at all, and Daniel was a kind person and more than willing to sort out his problems if he could.

'You'd better tell me the whole story,' he said, and Perceval, for that was his name, came and sat on the bed and began.

Percy told his story with lots of pauses for miserable sniffing and cries of 'Oh, what am I to do?' and 'I shall be alone forever!', so it took him quite a long time.

Percy and his parents, Ronald and Iphigenia, had materialized in good time at the service station, where they had met up with Cousin Vera and the other ghosts and spectres who had applied for Mountwood School for Ghosts. There was quite a crowd milling about the parking bay where the bus was to pick them up. Some of them were old acquaintances, and they hung about, chatting, catching up on each other's news. After a while, when the bus still hadn't come, Percy had got bored and wandered off. There were lots of great big lorries standing silent and dark in the parking area. Percy glided among them, peeping in sometimes to look at the drivers snoring in their cabs. They had little beds with curtains, which reminded Percy of when he had been alive and his mother had read poetry to him before he went to sleep. His favourite one had started, 'Where the bee sucks there suck I.'

When Percy got back to the pick-up place, he saw a bus standing in the parking bay, revving its engine. There were no ghosts to be seen. He cried, 'Help, help, wait for me! Don't leave without me!' and threw himself through the side of the bus just as it drew away and rumbled off into the night.

'But it wasn't a bus,' said Percy sadly, looking with at Daniel with tragic eyes. 'The bus had already left.'

'Well, why didn't your parents wait for you? They must have been worried sick when you didn't show up.'

'I don't know, I don't know. I have been aba . . . adn . . .'

'Abandoned.'

'Y-y-yes. Like the Babes in the Wood.' Percy collapsed in hopeless weeping.

When he had recovered slightly Daniel said, 'I still don't see how you could mistake a removal van for a bus.'

'But I've never *been* on a bus. And it had words on the side like where we were going.'

'What do you mean?'

But Percy could speak no more. With a final wail

of 'Poor me! Oh, sad unhappy me!' he threw himself face down on the bed.

Daniel heard Great-Aunt Joyce's bedroom door opening, and her tread on the stair.

'That's done it,' he said.

'I'll disappear,' said Percy. 'I'm quite good at it.' And he started to fade, vanishing just as Great-Aunt Joyce appeared in the doorway.

Daniel turned on his bedside light. Great-Aunt Joyce was wearing a flannel dressing gown and tartan slippers, and her hair was in curlers. She looked very angry, and peered around the room.

'Really, Daniel, this is appalling. What on earth is going on? I must have silence after my pill. I shall be speaking to your father.'

'Oh, it's you, Great-Aunt Joyce. I was having a terrible nightmare.'

'Were you now?' said Great-Aunt Joyce suspiciously, and it seemed to Daniel that she stared intently at the exact spot where Percy had just vanished. 'A nightmare, was it? That's what comes of not chewing your food properly. Poor digestion.'

When she had gone, a small voice spoke from the empty bed.

'She doesn't seem very nice,' said Percy.

'She isn't. We'll have to be absolutely quiet now, Percy. We'll talk about this tomorrow.'

THE BEASTS OF CLAWSTONE CASTLE

EVA IBBOTSON

'They ought to be in the country,' said Mrs Hamilton.
'It's where children ought to be.'

When Madlyn Hamilton and her younger brother
Rollo are sent by their mother to stay with their
Uncle George at crumbling Clawstone Castle, they
can see that action is needed before the castle falls
down completely! With the help of a team of
scary ghosts – including Mr Smith, a one-eyed
skeleton, and Brenda the Bloodstained Bride – they
hatch a spooky plan to save their new home. But
with a sinister scientist after the estate's prize
cattle, money might not be enough to save the
mysterious white beasts of Clawstone Castle . . .

THE SECRET OF PLATFORM 13

EVA IBBOTSON

'Well, this is it!' said Ernie Hobbs, floating past the boarded-up Left Luggage Office and coming to rest on an old mailbag. 'This is the day!'

Platform 13 at King's Cross Station hides a remarkable secret. Every nine years a doorway opens to an amazing, fantastical island and its occupants come visiting. But the last time the doorway was open the island's baby prince was stolen from the streets of London. Now, nine years later, a rescue party, led by a wizard and an ogre, is back to find him and bring him home. But the gentle prince seems to have become a spoilt rich boy, and he doesn't believe in magic and *doesn't* want to go home. Can they rescue him before the doorway disappears forever?

WHICH WITCH?

EVA IBBOTSON

'And remember,' he said, throwing out his arms,
'that what I am looking for is power,
wickedness and evil. Darkness is All!'

Arriman the Awful, feared Wizard of the North, is
searching for a monstrous witch with the darkest
powers and is holding a sorcery competition to
discover which witch is the most fiendish.
Glamorous Madame Olympia conjures up a
thousand plague-bearing rats, while Belladonna,
the white witch, desperately wants to be a
wicked enchantress, but only manages to
produce flowers not snakes. Can she become
more devilish than all the other witches?